HURT *me*

Ali
Don't hurt me ♡ *Kdukey*

♡ *KWebster*

KER DUKEY & K WEBSTER

Hurt Me

This is a work of fiction. Names, characters, places, and incidents either are the product of the author's imagination or are used fictitiously, and any resemblance to actual persons, living or dead, business establishments, events, or locales is entirely coincidental.

From international bestselling authors, Ker Dukey and K Webster comes a fast-paced, hot, MM instalove standalone lunchtime read from their KKinky Reads collection!

I got my dream at a young age.
The lead singer of one of the most popular bands in the world—Berlin Scandal.
I'm a rock god.
But under the façade of living the dream, a twisted secret consumes me.

Angry lyrics and a brooding attitude propelled my career.
Getting wasted and lashing out behind the scenes could be my downfall.
I'm spiraling and don't know how to stop the descent.

Now, my record label has issued me a babysitter.
Blaine Mannford, a hardass detective with a dark thirst.
And he's looking at me like I can quench it.

He's not my type in more ways than one.
Bossy. Forceful. Firm. A man.
I don't like cops. I don't like him.

Unfortunately, he likes it when I fight him—enjoys punishing me how he sees fit.
I'm screwed up in the head, because I'm a willing player in his dirty game.
I want him to hurt me.

This is a steamy, kinky romance with a small amount of BDSM themes sure to make you blush! A perfect combination of sexy and intense you can devour in one sitting! You'll get a happy ending that'll make you swoon!

BOOKS BY
KER DUKEY

Empathy Series:
Empathy
Desolate
Vacant—Novella
Deadly—Novella

The Broken Series:
The Broken
The Broken Parts of Us
The Broken Tethers That Bind Us—Novella
The Broken Forever—Novella

The Men by Numbers Series:
Ten
Six

Drawn to You Duet:
Drawn to You
Lines Drawn

Standalone Novels:
My Soul Keeper
Lost
I See You
The Beats in Rift
Devil

BOOKS BY
K WEBSTER

Psychological Romance Standalones:

My Torin

Whispers and the Roars

Cold Cole Heart

Blue Hill Blood

Romantic Suspense Standalones:

Dirty Ugly Toy

El Malo

Notice

Sweet Jayne

The Road Back to Us

Surviving Harley

Love and Law

Moth to a Flame

Erased

Extremely Forbidden Romance Standalones:

The Wild

Hale

Like Dragonflies

2 Lovers Series:

Text 2 Lovers (Book 1)

Hate 2 Lovers (Book 2)

Thieves 2 Lovers (Book 3)

Pretty Little Dolls Series:

Pretty Stolen Dolls (Book 1)

Pretty Lost Dolls (Book 2)

Pretty New Doll (Book 3)

Pretty Broken Dolls (Book 4)

The V Games Series:

Vlad (Book 1)

Ven (Book 2)

Vas (Book 3)

Four Fathers Books:

Pearson

Four Sons Books:

Camden

Elite Seven Books:

Gluttony

Not Safe for Amazon Books:

The Wild

Hale

Bad Bad Bad

This is War, Baby

Like Dragonflies

The Breaking the Rules Series:
Broken (Book 1)
Wrong (Book 2)
Scarred (Book 3)
Mistake (Book 4)
Crushed (Book 5—a novella)

The Vegas Aces Series:
Rock Country (Book 1)
Rock Heart (Book 2)
Rock Bottom (Book 3)

The Becoming Her Series:
Becoming Lady Thomas (Book 1)
Becoming Countess Dumont (Book 2)
Becoming Mrs. Benedict (Book 3)

Alpha & Omega Duet:
Alpha & Omega (Book 1)
Omega & Love (Book 2)

Pain has never been more addictive than
when he's inflicting it.

For the ones who crave the sting of a whip.
The burn of a firm spank.
The ache of a bite.

Embrace the pain.
The hurt only makes the pleasure greater.

PROLOGUE

Blaine

Sweat drips from our overheated skin, the movements between us like a dance—skilled, fluid, powerful. Each thrust finds purchase, creating a game of stamina, strength, dominance. In sync, heavy breathing echoes through the room.

I need this release, this outlet. We lost an officer today—killed in the line of duty. My head clears with each beat of my racing heart. It's just the two of us. I give, he takes. I pound, pushing my body forward in powerful strokes.

"That's good," he tells me. "More."

I give him more—bam, bam, bam. He falters, feet stumbling backward. I drop my hands, gulping down some air. Bruises blossom on my partner's cheek, just as I know they are on my jaw. Sparring has become a tradition of sorts for us. Whenever the job gets bad, we come to the gym to beat the shit outta each other until we bleed out the ugly.

"You done?" I pull my gloves off and pat his back.

He answers by swiping at his lip and nodding.

"Drinks?" I ask, hoping he says *no*. I want to find myself a nice ass to sink into.

"Nah, Jess is cooking. You're welcome to come to dinner."

"Pass. I've had your wife's cooking before. Spent two days married to the toilet."

"I'll tell her you said that." He chuckles.

Showering and changing, I check the mirror for cuts, sealing one on my brow with some tape before heading out.

The bar is hopping. Fridays nights are always busy. I like the noise that fills my head.

I flag down the bartender and order a couple chasers and a beer, checking my phone while I wait. I fire off a text to Ronan, and his brother, Ren, to ask if they are coming in tonight. This place is owned by Ronan's girl, and she likes to make appearances to keep the crowds piling in. Sofina is a famous name these days, after Ronan, my best friend and label owner, launched her career. I get fast replies from them both. Ronan's working, and Ren sends a pic from inside Hush, a sex club our friend owns.

Ren: Got plans ;)

"What are you smiling about?" a masculine voice

croons, the owner of said voice sidling up to me and tipping his beer to my phone.

I recognize him from here. He's looked my way on more than one occasion, but never dared to approach me. I usually like to do the hunting, but tonight, I just want to fuck and sleep, so I drink the chasers the bartender places down and lift my chin to him.

"I was smiling at the thoughts running through my head of the ways I could destroy you," I challenge, a smirk playing at my lips.

He gulps, his eyes never leaving mine. He's tall and has a sturdy frame with toned muscles. Smooth features, a sweet, appealing face with shaggy brown hair—the surfer type. If I had to guess, I'd say early twenties. I like them young.

"Is that a promise or a challenge?" he asks, licking his lips.

"It was a warning." I grin. "Grab your coat."

We've been back at my place for five fucking minutes, and he's already irritating me by trying to top from the damn bottom.

"You wanna suck my dick?" he asks, rubbing his hand down the bulge in his jeans.

I narrow my eyes. "Have you earned my lips on your cock? Get fucking naked," I bark.

He's just about to drop his jeans when music blasts from his pocket. Familiar fucking music. I groan.

"Please tell me that's not your ringtone," I grunt.

He tucks a strand of hair behind his ear, looking sheepish, his cheeks flushed. "Berlin Scandal. I fucking love them. You know them? Their shit is pretty catchy." He grins, shoving his hand into his pocket to pull out his phone.

I fucking know them all right. Their lead singer is stalking my thoughts, haunting my fucking dreams. Xavi Jacobs—a mouthy, little shit who needs a firm hand to reign him in.

The boy in front of me taps over the screen, then Berlin Scandal's latest song starts over. Xavi's gravelly voice croons from the device, heating the air and making my dick grow.

"I have their album on Spotify," he tells me, waving his phone. "I like to fuck to music, but I can turn it off if you want."

Rolling my shoulders, I drop my jeans and yank my T-shirt over my head. My veins pump all the blood in my body to my dick. "No, leave it on and bend the fuck over."

1

Xavi

Heroin.

I won't touch that shit with a ten-foot pole. I owe that much to Lex. It stole him from my bandmate, Owen, and me. Owen's little brother and my best friend overdosed. He left us shredded and raw. Exposed to the public, our wounds bleeding for all to see.

Scrubbing my palm over my face, I try desperately to keep the pain locked tight in the cavernous hollow of my heart. When I'm here—with them—I don't want them to see I die a little every fucking day without him.

I hate you, Lex.

The thought is like bitter sludge creeping through my veins, infecting me worse than any wicked hit of the brown.

I don't hate him. I never could. That's why he died. Because I couldn't fucking tell him no. I couldn't fucking get him to see he was slowly killing himself.

And now, without him, I'm the one dying.

Music thumps, buzzing through me, reminding me I'm not alone in my massive house. There are hundreds of goddamn people milling about. Berlin Scandal is the hottest alternative band this country has seen since the 90s when Nirvana ruled the charts. Our grungy style is considered "a homage to the past." We've opened for big acts like Pearl Jam, Alice in Chains, and Foo Fighters, who are still killing it despite doing this shit for decades. Where they're holding onto their old fan base who are my parents' age, Berlin Scandal is raking in all the Harry Styles and teeny bopper kids fanatical over our dark vibe.

We're different, but familiar.

Sellable as fuck.

Thanks to Harose Records.

Irritation churns in my gut. Ren Hayes wooed the hell out of us. Showed up at nearly every gig, praising and fucking worshiping us. Owen, our lead guitarist, begged me, Seth, and Riley into signing with Harose. We were all still raw over Lex and caved.

Money.

We're fucking rolling in it, and have been since we scribbled our names on the dotted lines. We've toured twenty-six states in a matter of months. Our debut album, *Hurt Me*, has gone platinum three times as millions of people across the globe obsess over our music.

This is everything we ever dreamed of.

What we wanted from the get-go.

We're rich, popular, and get our dicks sucked sometimes three times a night.

Everyone is happy…except me.

Owen can push the death of his brother two years ago into a hole and stomp on the lid to keep it shut, but I'm not wired that way. With each song I write and lyric I belt into the microphone, I relive the hurt of the night he left me. The pain is barbed wire wrapped around my heart, piercing into the broken organ and bleeding it dry. Each day is worse than the last. I'd do anything to numb the constant ache inside me, even if it means creating pain on the outside.

I grab my pack of smokes before yanking one out and pressing it between my lips. I flip open my Zippo—one Lex gave me—and study the flame as my cigarette dangles from my lips. Hot. Orange. Bright. His old party trick was to hold the flame to his flesh as long as he could and prove what a badass he was. Lighting my cigarette, I suck in the soothing, tainted air, then hold out my palm to tease the flame of the Zippo beneath my pink flesh. Searing hot pain erupts over my palm, sending warning signals racing up my nerve endings.

I don't flee.

I don't stop.

I watch it burn.

When hot tears sting my eyes, I blink them back and snap the Zippo shut. It still has the stupid Chiquita banana sticker Lex stuck on it. On one edge, it's bent over and no longer sticky. I rub at it with my thumb to press it back down, but it doesn't stay.

I smoke the hell out of my cigarette, until it goes out. Stubbing it out on my forearm, I flick the butt and stare at my palm.

My hand fucking hurts, and the skin is bubbled.

Too long.

Sometimes, I leave the flame on too long and fuck myself up more than I intend. But because I'm filthy fucking rich now, I have discreet doctors—both the mental and physical kind—who keep me loaded up on any medicinal shit I might need. With a heavy sigh, I stalk into the bathroom in my room and locate the cream I use for these instances. Slathering it on, I grit my teeth. At least I'm not thinking about the gaping wound inside me. I find some gauze and roll it around my hand before securing it with tape.

Owen's going to be pissed.

We have a photoshoot in the morning downtown with GQ. Some new-age rock star bullshit magazine spread—something the label is forcing us to do.

Every time I think about Harose, it makes me think of Ronan Hayes. I like Ren just as much as the rest of our band and signed the stupid contract, but I have serious beef with his brother, Ronan.

Unease trickles through me. I won't admit why I have issues with him, not even to myself. He just pushes his fist inside my heart and stirs up shit that's best kept hidden. It makes me hate him with every ounce of my being. Like the spoiled fucking brat I am, it makes me want to taunt him—ruin him like his very existence ruins me.

I kind of enjoyed irritating him by acting out and not being his perfect band singer.

But then he called in backup.

Six-foot three. Stacked as hell. A fucking monster with a badge. Ronan only made me loathe him more, because calling in backup for my "little boy tantrums" only confused me.

Confused.

I hate that fucking word.

They use it for people trying to understand their sexuality. I don't need to figure mine out. I was just fine fucking anything with a pair of tits until Lex overdosed and stole my goddamn soul. I was eighteen when I lost him—barely got to spend any time with him in this life. Now, when I see someone who reminds me of my best friend, I have the urge to yank them to me so I can press a thousand damn kisses to their mouth.

That's confusing, yes.

But what really burns me up is it's not just the rare, lanky guy with a lazy smile. It's guys like Ronan and Asshole Cop. That part's not confusing, it's infuriating.

I'm not attracted to men.

I just miss my best friend.

And because of his death, I'm drawn to guys like him. My heart begs to get a glimpse of Lex within each one. It's cruel and unusual torture. If I didn't think Dr. Maggs would shove more unnecessary drugs down my throat, I'd ask him to help me get these maddening thoughts out of my head.

But what if he tells someone?

My entire career is based on the fact that I'm a sex god who sings like a fucking dark angel. Girls—by the hundreds of thousands—cry and collapse when they see us. It's fucking strange and oddly empowering. What happens when they find out I'm ungrateful? That I wish they were a hundred thousand Lex looka-likes instead? That sometimes I get hot thinking about Ronan yelling at me and throwing shit in his rage. Or that I've jacked off more times than I can count to the memory of Asshole Cop manhandling me into sub-mission any time I lose it at Ronan's office.

I'm fucked.

I'm not gay or confused.

Just fucked in the head.

I storm out of the bathroom and dig around in my

nightstand until I find some mollies. In the past, two or three would get me nice and loose, but now, I require more. I choke down four and chase them with an open bottle of Jack. As soon as my skin starts to tingle, I abandon Jack and exit the safe confines of my room to find pussy—my other drug of choice.

"Oh, God," a girl yells out as soon as I leave the wing of my house that's off limits and join the party. "Look at him! Look at him!"

I glance toward the sound of her voice and size her up. Short. Big tits. Nice wide hips to hold onto. The pink fabric of her leggings stretches over her thick thighs, and I want to tear them off with my teeth.

Fuck yes.

This is me.

Finding a nice piece of ass who worships the ground I walk on to drive my dick into. Not whatever the fuck I was twenty minutes ago.

Pink Leggings Girl beams at me, jiggling her fat tits as she bounces in place. She pulls out her phone and starts recording as she chants, "Omigodomigodomigod."

Flashing her a lazy grin, I saunter over to her and pose. Tomorrow, this video will be all over social media—one more thing for my parents to lecture me about whenever they call.

"I like your tits," I say with a wicked grin. "Songs are written about tits like yours." I reach between us and rub my fingers over the front of her leggings between the juncture of her thighs. "Your thighs, though, are what wars are fought over."

The girl fucking swoons on her feet, nearly dropping her phone.

"Turn off the phone and play with me," I taunt as I grip her wrist and drag her behind me through the crowd.

Pink Leggings Girl loses the phone in her cleavage to latch herself to me. I pass Owen on a sofa. Some brunette bitch is riding him buck-ass naked in front of everyone. Riley is passed out, already in a recliner like an old man, his drumsticks hugged to his chest like they might run away in his sleep. Seth will be ready to party, though. I can always count on our bassist to get fucked up with me.

I find him outside by my pool, emphatically telling a story, his massive tattooed arms waving wildly around him. Coke dusts his nose. He's flying as high as a fucking kite. I give Pink Leggings Girl a little tweak to her nipple through her shirt before meeting with my boy.

"Zaveeeeeeee," he calls out, launching himself at me for a bear hug. When we first met as teens, he kept fucking up the pronunciation of my name. Xavi. Easy as fuck. But this motherfucker kept saying it like "Exavee." I got pissed and barked out "za" and then "vee." Even fucking wrote it down so he'd get it. Now, he calls me Zavee. Which is exactly how you say it, but I know this motherfucker sees it spelled the wrong way in his head.

"What's up, snowflake?" I slap my sore hand on his shoulder as we hug.

"We're rollin' hard tonight waiting on your lazy ass."

He pulls away slightly to grin at me. His shirt is missing, and he's sweating like a damn pig. Every woman in this place salivates over his tattoos and muscles. Seth's the body of our group. The one all the girls want to fuck. I'm the face—the one they all want to look up at while they suck cock. Owen's clearly the dick and our fearless leader, and Riley? I don't know what the fuck Riley is.

I drag my eyes down his front, wishing I had half the muscle mass he does. When he's not getting fucked up, he works out hard. My lazy ass just watches. Thank fuck I was born with good genes. My workout is the stage when I play guitar with Owen and sing my fucking soul out.

"You and your girl come to party?" He throws his arm over my shoulders so he can check out Pink Leggings Girl.

She blushes and gazes at us with stars in her eyes.

Seth whistles at her. "Damn, sweetheart, you are lookin' fine in those bubblegum pants. My boy here likes to share." He looks up at me, smirking. We've fucked the same woman a time or two. Okay, so maybe more than two.

"Um, yeah?" she says, beaming. "I'm down for whatever. I love you guys. I've been obsessed with you both since I heard your first song."

"And you haven't even seen Zavee's pretty dick yet, doll," Seth says with a laugh as he boldly grabs it through my jeans. "Aw, he's hard too. My boy's always hard and ready to fuck."

I shove his hand off my cock. "She's mine tonight," I snap, anger surging up inside me. "Go find your own piece of ass."

The girl smiles shyly at me, like I just told her she's the one and I'm going to fucking marry her. Truth is, I don't trust myself right now. Not with Seth looking like a fucking snack and grabbing on my cock like he owns it.

Seth plays off my anger and grabs my arm to guide me over to a table. He nods at one of the guys chopping some blow with a razor. Needing the fire, I lean forward, snorting a line from the plate. Seth slaps my ass, laughing, and I fucking explode.

Swirling around, I clock him right in the fucking face. He may be bigger than me, but he's stunned by my aggression. Blood spurts from his nose, and my first thought is how pissed Ronan will be that I fucked Seth's face up before our photoshoot tomorrow.

Seth, raging like a bull, charges. He slams into me,

knocking me hard to the ground. His fist hits my ribs, and pain slices through me. I manage to flip him over and glance up in time to see Pink Leggings Girl filming me again. I grin at the camera.

BAM!

My vision goes black as Seth punches me. I'm about to swing again when two guys rush us. Owen starts yelling at Seth while Riley steps between us. Seth and I are both hellbent on getting to the other, but Owen and Riley—the only two people who truly care about us—prevent that from happening.

"What the actual fuck?" Owen demands, his pants hanging open where he's barely pulled them up over his still hard dick after his getting laid in my living room. One of his hands is on Seth's chest, pushing him away from me.

I drag my eyes from the visible part of Owen's cock and hate myself for wondering what he smells like there. Who the fuck wonders that shit?

Riley holds me back when I start forward, my eyes latching on Seth's. Regret washes over his features. It'll be all over social media in the morning and we both know it. When I hear sirens, Owen curses.

"Come on," Riley growls. "Let's get you out of here."

I break from his hold. My body is buzzing from the drugs and my fists ache to pummel Seth some more. But my eyes keep sliding to Owen's dick. Dark, trimmed hair. Tattoos all over his lower abdomen. Did Lex have the same cock?

Pain assaults me from the inside out, exploding like a bomb.

I charge for Owen, hellbent on making him pay too. I've barely raised my fist before Riley yanks me back. My foot swings out, and I clip Owen in the nuts with my boot. He howls, then charges, sending me and Riley splashing into the pool. The cold water is a wakeup call as we sputter and swim to the surface.

So many phones.

Everywhere.

How do I explain this to Mom and Dad?

And Ronan.

Holy shit...and Asshole Cop.

I wish I could fucking drown right now.

2

Blaine

Pulling up to my condo after working fifteen hours straight, I debate ignoring the ringing of my cell phone. Ronan's name flashes like a warning, and despite my need for sleep, I answer.

"What's up, Hayes? Don't you know what time it is? Shouldn't you be curled around your little girl sleeping like a baby?"

His deep chuckle fades into a groggy growl, "Yeah, that's exactly what I should be doing, but that punk-ass motherfucker is being live-streamed brawling with his bandmates."

An internal snarl rumbles my chest. I pinch the top of my nose to ease the tired ache. "I'll cool things over." I exhale on a frustrated breath.

"I owe you." He sighs.

"You always owe me. One day, I'll collect," I grunt,

grinning. He knows I'm lying. Ronan Hayes is my best friend and would do anything for me. I'll do him this favor—and the next when it arises.

The punk-ass motherfucker in question is Xavi Jacobs. A guy propelled into stardom at a real young age. The kid is fucking troubled, which is leading him into trouble. He's acting out. It's a fucking cry for help if I ever saw one. But it's tough to get through to entitled fuckers like him. Ronan's patience is wearing real thin. If Berlin Scandal didn't make a fuck load of money for his record label, he'd drop them like hot coal.

I've had to babysit this kid before.

His eyes are full of pain.

A dark cloud of sorrow and regret follow him around, drenching him in misery.

I've seen it so many times before. He's burdened and needs a way to release the hurt. Self-sabotage is his weapon of choice. It boils my blood watching someone so talented with the world at his feet act out so recklessly.

My palm twitches. I want to teach him how to release that pain in a way beneficial for him—pleasurable. Fuck! I need to get this kid out my head. There's something about him that calls to the depravity inside me—the Dom—the daddy—the sadist.

Pulling onto his street, I flash my badge at the security guy standing at the gate leading up to Xavi's mansion. He waves me in with a defeated shrug.

Red and blue lights flash across the dark night sky, and I groan. Someone called the cops, making this more of a ball ache than I anticipated.

Raised voices bark and screech over the blaring music as I get out of the truck. A crowd has gathered on the front lawn, flashes from cell phones flickering like fireflies as they capture clickbait images.

They call themselves friends or fans, but they're scavengers feeding on the carcasses of the band members they claim to worship. And their favorite is Xavi Jacobs.

I push through the throngs of people, moving toward bickering voices. Three people, facedown, being detained in handcuffs, come into view. Three quarters of the band.

"Where's Xavi?" I call out to O'Neil, a uniform I know from the precinct.

O'Neil's face contorts in confusion. "This is just a disturbing the peace complaint. No need for you to be here, sir," he assures me.

"I'll tell *you* where I need to be. Let them up," I tell him, nodding to the band eating dirt.

They're pulled to their feet. All but one of them is shirtless and soaking wet. Blood drips from the nose of the big fella, who I think plays bass. His brow crashes and jaw ticks with frustration. What a fucking mess.

"Where's Xavi?" I demand again.

Shaking his head, he growls, "He won't get out of the pool."

"He's out back with Davis," O'Neil grumbles, pointing to a side gate while un-cuffing the other guys.

"Clear these people out," I bark out. "And someone turn that fucking music off."

"Hey," the big guy spits out, "that's our music."

Smirking, I walk over to him, all six-foot-three, two hundred and forty pounds of muscle. He's big, but I'm bigger. Intimidation flickers in his eyes as I stand toe to toe with him.

"Keep this shit up, and the only music you'll be making is from a prison shower while the inmates decide which one gets to make you their bitch."

"It was Xavi." He lifts his chin. "He swung at me."

Xavi comes barreling through the gate wearing only a soaked pair of jeans, the top button undone, and no shoes. A wet, snapped cigarette hangs from his lips and an unraveling bandage flies like a twirling ribbon from his hand.

He laughs through pinched lips, looking over his shoulder at Officer Daniels, who's chasing him at a snail's pace, huffing and puffing. The fucker is older than all these guys combined. Xavi's eyes clash with mine, and his feet falter. He skids on the grass, almost falling face-first. Placing my hands on my hips, I glare at him. His shoulders deflate, realizing playtime is over.

"I've got this, Daniels," I tell the officer who waves a defeated hand in the air, bending to drag air into his burning lungs before he limps back to his squad car mumbling curses under his breath.

"Go get the place cleaned up," I tell the other band members. They groan, but do as their told. Good boys.

The place has been cleared of *adoring* fans, and the music is finally shut off. The yard is fucking trashed and not one asshole sticks around to offer to clean this shit up. Who needs enemies when you have friends who destroy your place and air your discrepancies online?

"Why do you make me come over here when I should be in bed right now?" I growl, snatching the cigarette from Xavi's mouth, dropping it to the ground, and crushing it under my boot.

He's glares at me with balls of steel. Xavi's a lot smaller than me, lean and natural. Where I lift and bulk up, his muscles are subtle and slender. Like a typical drugged-up rock star living his "best" life.

"I'm not stopping you from going to bed, Grandpa." He crosses his arms over his chest and grins, showing off a perfect set of white teeth stained from a cut on his lip. This kid needs discipline, and I crave to dish it out. My eyes focus on the crimson spilt in his bottom lip. I ache to bite him there—to push the burn and see if he breaks.

"Get in the fucking house before I lose my shit and they have to take me away in the squad car," I warn, pointing to the open door.

"We were fucking around," he gripes. "Some prick called the cops. It's a misunderstanding."

"You were being live-streamed acting like a fucking idiot. You're supposed to be a family, a band bonded through friendship. That's not the way best friends act. Do you even like each other?"

His features darken with fury.

"We love each other. We're brothers," he snaps as soon as we're inside, picking up a bottle of beer from a table and throwing it against the wall beside me. It shatters with a crash, and the shards rebound on contact, littering the room. His deep brown eyes widen as my face hardens.

I march toward him, grabbing him around the throat and pushing his back against a wall. I close in, drowning him with my size. He doesn't resist or attempt to release my grip. His Adam's apple bobs beneath my palm. Color tints his cheeks. This turns him on. Heat roars through me, demanding attention. Pushing my thumb against the spilt on his lip, I smirk when he gasps and his pupils dilate. Blood blooms and coats the pad of my thumb. Delicious.

"I think you just want me to put you in my cuffs," I taunt, pushing into him until we're flush against the other.

"Fuck you," he mumbles past the pressure I'm applying there with my thumb.

"*I* do the fucking, boy. Keep giving me this lip, and I'll fuck that pretty mouth of yours just to shut you up."

His body goes rigid—even his cock. A storm rages in his eyes, and then the spell is broken when a girl in pink tights with tits spilling from her top that's too small for her build comes through the front door, distracting us both. "Oh, I'm sorry, officer." She startles when she sees us. "I just wanted to give Xavi his cell phone. It got knocked from his pocket when the whole fight thing started." She shrugs.

I take it from her, releasing Xavi. "Thanks, darling." I wink, and a crimson blush blooms on her cheeks.

"I put my number in there, Xavi. Call me?" She bites her lip and waves before leaving.

Swiping the screen, I'm granted access. I shake my head in astonishment. "You don't lock your phone?"

"Why would I?" he argues in a petulant way that's going to earn him punishment one day—from me. "It's usually only me who has it."

"Until you do stupid shit like lose it while hitting your fucking bandmates because you have a chip on your shoulder and won't admit you need help," I growl, fury rippling through me.

How fucking stupid can he be?

These people just want to use and abuse him.

He's entertainment to them. Not a person. A fucking show—a shitshow at that.

"I don't need help. I'm twenty years old. Rich and famous. Being a fuck-up is exactly what I'm supposed to be doing."

Laughing, I pin him with a narrowed stare. "You think getting everything you want in life entitles you to be a dick?"

"Who said this is everything I want?" he snaps, swiping the cell from my hands. "You shouldn't assume shit, Detective."

I take a calming breath, pinning him in place with my intense stare. Beneath the angry exterior is a very broken boy. He needs someone to put him back together.

"Go make peace with your band. Ronan's going to have to make miracles happen to fix this mess."

"Are you just going to show up every time I fuck up?" He smirks, folding his arms over his chest. Wet strands of curled hair hang down over his face. I want to fist it in my hands.

Licking my lips, I run my gaze up his body. He squirms. "Is that why you keep getting into trouble? In hopes I'll come discipline you?" I mutter in a deep growl.

His jaw tenses and his arms drop, hands curling into fists. "What? No," he huffs out in a defensive tone. "Why the fuck would I want that?"

Because it's written all over your damn face.

"Calm down, boy. I'm just fucking with you." I smirk. "Are you going to behave if I leave? I don't want to be called back out here for this juvenile shit. When I make early hour house calls, I expect to be inflicting the carnage, not cleaning it up." I raise a brow in challenge.

His features furrow, trying to figure out what I mean. He'll find out one day—when he's ready to admit to himself why he's lashing out all the damn time.

He concedes with a nod, but doesn't meet my penetrating stare anymore. "I'm going to sleep it off. I'll talk to everyone in the morning."

"Good plan. Sweet dreams." With that, I leave him. I slipped my number in his phone when Pink Tights gave it to me. Next time he's feeling weird and wants to act out, hopefully he'll think twice and call me.

I climb into my truck and call Ronan. He picks up on the second ring. That poor bastard didn't get to go back to sleep.

"Hey, what's happening?" He exhales heavily.

"I've cleared the house out. They're going to sleep it off. You'll need to do some press control and get them out in the public eye together—a united front—as soon as possible."

"Already on it. That fucker makes me lose too much sleep. He's out of control," he grinds out.

"He's hurting, Ronan. He needs therapy."

"He needs a firm hand." Ronan snorts.

"Well, that too." I grin, despite him not being able to see me.

"What do you suggest?"

"I'll do what I can," I assure him. "Just leave it with me."

I end the call and wait for the lights inside to shut off before I drive my tired ass home.

3

Xavi

"Ruined!" the stylist complains the moment all four of us heathens walk into the GQ studio. "Where's Marcus? Someone get me Marcus!"

Seth smirks. "This is your fault, Zavee."

We're battered and bruised and hungover as fuck. Definitely my fault. At least my bandmates are used to my shit. Seth was quickest to forgive, followed by Riley. Owen is speaking to me, but he's still pissed.

"We look edgy," I argue, shrugging.

"Edgy, young, and dumb," a deep voice rumbles from behind us. "Still sellable, thank fuck."

Ren Hayes strides over to us, clasping me on the shoulder. "You assholes are all over social media. I've been on a Twitter frenzy saving your asses." He's smiling—which is good. Smiling is definitely good.

"We're brothers. We fight," I state like it's nothing.

23

Brothers don't get turned on by each other then get pissed over it. They may be brothers to me, but last night, fueled by alcohol, my stupid body reacted to Owen's half naked state. He looks so damn much like his brother, it's painful at times. I wasn't thinking clearly because of the toxic shit running through my veins—nothing more.

I'm not gay.

So why the hell am I acting like it?

While Ren discusses his strategy to spin our fight into something he can use, I break off from the group and plop down in a chair. I check social media and inwardly cringe. It fucking sucks we're always on display. There's always some "groupie" waiting to capture all the moments. Good and bad. Mostly bad. I miss the days when we'd rock out in Lex and Owen's garage. Riley would beat on the drums, annoying the shit out of every adult in a one-mile radius. Lex didn't have a musical bone in his body, but he was our official mascot.

And official drug dealer.

Fuck, we spun out of control so fast. Especially him. Where we focused on the music and making demos to send to labels. He focused on getting high. My best friend went down while we went up. And then he stayed down. Six-feet under.

Pain numbs me. The urge to hunt down a bar is strong. Instead, I pull out my Zippo.

Flick.

Burn.

The orange flame dances under the vent of the air conditioner above me, threatening to blow out. Kind of like me. Just barely hanging on while everything works against me. I snap the lighter shut and rub the sticker down again.

God, I miss him.

Someone laughs from nearby, stealing me from my melancholy. Owen—as unofficial leader of our band—waves his hands in the air as he explains his newest idea to Ren. I stare at him for a long time, just taking a moment to drink how much he looks like Lex. Riley shoots me a sympathetic smile. Seth playfully flips me off.

I can't believe we fucking fought.

In front of everyone.

I don't deserve them. They'd do so much better with a more responsible front man. One who isn't so fucked in the head. One who doesn't hate himself and the life he's graciously been given.

My mind drifts to Asshole Cop, otherwise known as Blaine. He gets under my skin like Ronan does. But where Ronan flips his shit and wants to explode on me, Blaine acts like he wants to possess me. His dark brown eyes don't just look at me, they look into me. Through me. Inspect every cell inside me. It's intrusive as fuck. I hate that he has that ability.

I don't want to be seen.

Yes, you do.

What I hate more is the way my body lights up like the flame from my Zippo. Instead of scarring my flesh and grounding me, he burns me from the inside out, incinerating my very being. It's fucking maddening.

I can't help but remember the way he grabbed my throat and pushed me against the wall. If I were smart, I would've been intimidated by his sheer strength and size. The dude could break me with a snap of his wrist.

But he didn't break me.

He held me in place, his body heating mine and eyes penetrating me. They made promises—promises I had no hope of interpreting. Threats and warnings. If I kept my shit up, he'd *make* me behave. My dick jolts in my jeans and anger surges through me.

Fuck him.

He's not my dad.

He doesn't sign my checks.

The guy's a fuckin' cop with an attitude. Probably goes home each night and jerks off to videos of me singing. He doesn't get to touch me or mold me or fucking tell me what to do. I'm not his, nor will I ever be. His eyes told a story—one that said he'd love nothing more than to bend me over and take my ass. Gay was written all over the way he pinned me in a dominating way. *Well, motherfucker, too damn bad.* I bat for the other team. I'm into chicks with fat tits, slick cunts, and tight leather molded to their round asses. I like hair I can grab onto and a perfumed neck I can suck on.

I don't want muscles and scruff.

I don't fucking need a cock. Already got one.

And still…I can't get it out of my head—the way he pinned me—the control that radiated from him—his desire to possess and own me.

He had the power to do it too.

"Let's get this shit over with," I bark out. "I'm ready to get drunk, and you assholes are coming with me."

We're at some swanky as shit bar our dumb asses don't belong in. Stirring up trouble. It's what we do. These fuckers are rich as hell. Like us. But they don't think we belong here.

Their wives fucking do.

I wink at a blonde with huge tits spilling out of her expensive red dress. She has her hand around her wimpy husband's bicep, but her cheeks redden when our eyes lock. I make sure to eye-fuck her tits so she doesn't misinterpret my intentions.

Yeah, sweetheart. If you want a good time, follow us to the VIP lounge.

She bites on her plump red lip, considering my silent offer, but her husband drags her in the opposite direction, spoiling my fucking fun. Too bad. I'd have let her suck my dick. I'd have let her husband watch too. He looks like the cuckold type. Fucking pansy.

By the time we reach the roped-off VIP section, both Owen and Seth have collected women along the way. Riley hangs back with me, shrugging off the advances of a few women. It makes me wonder if he's gay. He doesn't get with women a lot. I've never seen him with a man, though.

Why do I care if he's gay?

I don't.

He can be whatever the fuck he wants to be as long as I don't have to watch him dick it to some dude. *What would Owen say?*

As soon as we make it into the private space, I head for the bar. The bartender is a guy close to my age. He grins when he sees me.

"Berlin Scandal," he says. "No way. You guys are my fucking idols."

I smile back. "Oh yeah? What's your favorite song?"

His green eyes drop to my lips for a moment and he leans forward. "'Into the Fire.' The lyrics are amazing."

"Into the Fire" is one of my favorites. It's a tribute to Lex.

"Good choice," I agree. "Get me the good shit. I'm getting fucked up tonight."

His smile goes wider. "I'm Devon. Whatever you want, I can get it. *Anything.*" A knowing smirk plays at his lips. "All you have to do is ask, Xavi."

I like this guy already.

"Let's start with a round for my band. And then you can show me the top shelf stuff a little later." I nod, dropping a credit card on the bar and sliding it toward him. "Have one yourself, yeah? Or two." I wink, knowing full well if I worked here with the rich bastards flashing their credit cards I'd be skimming a nice tip off the top.

His eyes widen in surprise. "Thanks…I'll definitely show you the good stuff later." He smirks.

I bet they keep some special shit in the back they only bring out when the real famous people show up.

He leaves me to go make a drink. When he comes back, his entire demeanor has changed. Sliding the shot my way, his stare lingers, dissecting me.

Green eyes flicker with interest as he darts them to my mouth. "You want the good stuff? I have some really good stuff. If you're still standing later, I'll bring it?"

Sounds like a goddamn challenge. I don't ever back down from those.

"Oh, I'll be the one still standing later." I knock back the shot and slam it on the bar. "Keep these coming, Green Eyes." *What the fuck did he say his name was again?*

He rewards me with a wide smile. "You got it."

After about the sixth shot, I glance around to see what my brothers are up to. Riley is in a heated discussion with a couple dudes in suits. Seth is telling a loud ass story, his voice traveling above the music. Owen has his tongue down a redhead's throat. Business as usual.

"I get off at two," the green-eyed bartender tells me, pushing another shot my way.

So?

Do I look like I need a play-by-play of his schedule?

"Cool, man," I utter, sucking down another shot. He was right, this shit is good.

"We could continue this party later. At my place," he offers. His palm opens, and a couple familiar happy pills smile back at me.

"Thanks, er, Deacon?" I take the pills from him and swallow them dry. "As long as Owen can bring his bitches, he'll go anywhere."

"Devon," he corrects with a grin. His attention slides over to Owen before darting back to my mouth. Seriously. What the fuck? Do I have some shit on my mouth?

"He can have his women, so long as I get you all to myself." He walks away to serve another drink, and I stare at him in confusion. When he senses me looking, he turns and winks at me.

Wait.

Is this fucking guy into me?

I'm backpedaling at warped speed as I look at the entire night with new eyes. This fucker's been flirting with me. I didn't even realize it. Hell, it could be misinterpreted that I flirted back. The E is buzzing through my veins, and my dick is thickening beyond my control. I check out the tattoos on Devon's neck, and Blaine the party pooper pops in my head. I rake my gaze down over him. He has a solid back like Blaine, leading down to a firm ass in his black pants. Holy fuck. No. No! What the fuck am I thinking? Fuck! There's something wrong with me.

Devon saunters back over to me and pours another shot into a glass. I reach for the bottle instead. His grip on it is tight, so my hand just holds onto his.

"I could lose my job if I give you this bottle," he says, frowning. "Just let me pour you a drink and I promise I'll take care of you better when we get home."

I jerk back my hand, heat burning through me. Anger. Rage. Fury. Shame. Lust. Fuck no. Fuck no. Fuck no.

"I gotta take a piss," I slur out, eager to get away from him and the wrong as hell impression he has about me. I down the shot, then stagger away.

KER DUKEY & K WEBSTER

As I push into the bathroom, someone follows me in. I swivel around, ready to whip some ass, but stop short. It's Devon. His eyes are on fire as he closes in on me. Shock paralyzes me as his hands grip my face and his lips press to mine. Because of the E and the fucking alcohol, I stand stock-still while his tongue prods at my mouth to open for him.

But my wrecked mind goes fucking crazy.

"What the hell is wrong with you?" I snarl with a shove, sending him stumbling back. "Do I look fucking gay to you?"

His green eyes widen. "You flirted with me all night, man. I caught you checking me out. Of course I thought you were fucking gay."

"I wasn't checking you out," I bellow, charging for him. "I'm not gay, asshole."

I shove him again, and he shoves me back.

"I fucking idolize you, dude, but not this. I don't need this shit in my life," he mutters, shaking me off. "You need to take a hard look at yourself, Xavi. What you see is not what everyone else sees."

What the hell does that mean?

I swing at him, but he ducks out of the way before storming out of the bathroom. I'm a raging bull and slip into one of the stalls to calm my thoughts so I don't destroy the entire club. My first instinct is to check social media. To see if he's telling the whole fucking world I've been flirting with him. I fucking wasn't...right?

Panic seizes me as I fly through each account, searching for any hint of my encounter with Devon. On Twitter, I find a picture someone took of me at the bar smiling at Devon with the hashtag #IWantInOnThatSandwich.

I screenshot it and text it to Ren. That shit freaks me out. People will run with it, and then what? What the hell happens?

Me: Make this go away.

Ren: What?

Me: This gay bullshit!

Ren: You're having a drink at a bar. There's nothing gay about that. You okay?

Me: When I kick Devon's ass, there'll be something wrong with that!

Ren: Xavi, calm your shit. Who is Devon?

Me: The guy in the picture.

Ren: The bartender? There's a million pictures every day of celebrities propped on a bar, Xavi. Why are you freaking out? Stop self-medicating on pills. It's making you paranoid.

Whatever, man.

I storm out of the bathroom and down the hallway to the alley around the back of the building. As soon as I'm free of the suffocating confines of the club, I suck in gulps of air.

I'm going to beat Devon's ass.

Punch his pretty boy face in.

Fuck, I'm a dick.

It's not his fault.

I'm losing my goddamn mind.

My phone buzzes, and I swipe it open to find a text from Blaine. Blaine? When the hell did I get his number and put it in my phone?

Blaine: Ren says you're having a meltdown.

What the fuck?

Me: Some guy just tried to make out with me in the bathroom. I'm going to kill him. Oops, probably better not to admit that to a damn cop.

Blaine: You're not going to touch him.

Anger explodes inside me. I kick the dumpster, letting loose a roar of frustration.

Me: You're not in charge of me!

Blaine: Stop being a brat and listen. You're going to sit your ass down right now and wait for me.

Heat chases away the anger, licking at my balls like a horny bitch.

Me: Fuck you.

Blaine: Don't say things you can't handle.

I blink in shock.

Me: I'm not into men, asshole.

Blaine: And I'm not in the mood to deal with your shit, boy, but here we are.

Me: You're really coming here? To do what? Handcuff me?

Blaine: For as much as you throw that in my face, I'm starting to think you want it.

Me: Fuck you.

Blaine: Keep it up, boy. Keep it the fuck up.

My cock jolts at his words. It's certainly up all right.

Me: I don't need you to come solve my problems.

Blaine: You sure as hell can't handle them on your own. Address. Now.

God, he's bossy as fuck. I want to fight him on this, but mostly, I want to get the hell out of here. If I go back in there, I'm going to punch Devon and ruin everyone's night. I already ruined last night. I sure as hell don't want to make a habit of this.

Defeated, I give him the name of the club and tell him I'm sitting in front of the dumpster. Like trash. How fucking appropriate. I lean against the metal and pull out my Zippo.

Flick. Burn.

Flick. Burn.

I open and close the lighter, staring at the flame. In the dark, alone, with the fucking Calvary on its way, it flames brighter and hotter. I pinch the orange flame with my thumb and finger, hissing at the sting. Snapping the lighter closed, I lick my wounded fingers.

I can't believe I just told a cop where I'm at. I'm wasted, fucked up on E, and pissed as hell—and I gave him directions to come to me. If that's not the definition of stupid, I don't know what is. If Lex were here, he'd thump me in the head and call me a dumb shit.

Fuck.

Why Lex?

Why'd you have to leave me?

You were my best friend.

My chest aches. Would we have stayed best friends, or would it have evolved into more? If Lex would have kissed me, would I have let him?

I don't like analyzing that shit. It's in the past, and it doesn't matter. He's fucking dead. I can be gayer than a bucket of rainbows, but it still won't raise him from the dead so I can lock lips with him.

Aching pain radiates inside me, killing the only parts left living. One day, I'm afraid it'll consume me altogether. I don't know what happens then. It's fucking terrifying.

Needing a break from my inner turmoil, I flip open my Zippo again.

Flick. Burn.

The flame sizzles my arm hair as I hold it against my forearm. It hurts, but steals my focus. All my thoughts and emotions are erased as I harness the pain and get high from it. When I can't take it anymore, I close the lighter and lay on the gravel. The world spins around me, so I close my eyes. My forearm throbs, and I let it beat through me like the cadence of Riley's drums. In my head, I make up lyrics for it. Move around the words attached to feelings and string them up in a pattern. No longer chaos inside, but music. A song. A reason. My deep voice rumbles as I hum along the notes forming.

The chaos is all-consuming.

One day, if I can't latch onto it and make it work for me in the form of music, what happens? Do I go fucking crazy from all the maddening thoughts? If only Lex could see me now, curled up on my side in front of a dumpster, humming a song only I know while praying for motherfucking peace.

I'm pathetic.

Twisted and lost.

I need help.

Shakily, I lift my Zippo.

Flick. Burn.

The flame scorches my wrist until a hot tear leaks from the corner of my eyes, forcing me to drop the Zippo.

I need fucking help.

4

Blaine

Hush, a sex club owned by a good friend of mine, is where I come when I need to let the beast loose. Willing playmates line up to sate my dark cravings here. Yet, tonight, I can't seem to get myself in the right headspace. I'm preoccupied with a particular fucker who just happens to be blasting through the stereo system with his new song flying high in the charts right now.

I hate that I know that. Know what songs are his, how well he's doing, what he's doing, where he's doing it. Am I the hunter or am I the fucking prey?

I should be focused on my new case, but I'm far from fucking focused lately. My mind is storming like a raging ocean ready to crash to shore to see if a certain boy can handle the wave I'm ready to drench him in.

The lyrics croon from the room, teasing me, his voice caressing the place in a sexy undertone, setting the mood. It reminds me of the pumping of my pulse after a rough fuck, and I can't stop thinking about having that boy pinned against the wall.

His broken, self-destructive attitude speaks to the healer inside me—to the detective driven to dissecting and finding a satisfactory resolution. But that fucking smirk and disobedient spark speaks to the Dom I am. Makes me want to cuff him, teach him all the ways I can bring him to his knees and make him beg for my firm punishment.

"Another?" Ren pipes up, reminding me I'm not alone.

I tip my beer bottle to my lips and drain the last of the liquid. "Nah, I want to keep a clear head."

He's fucking smirking. I can feel it in his tone when he says, "Big plans tonight? Levi has been eye-fucking you since you sat your ass down." I follow the path of his gaze to Levi, the bartender who has been trying to get *me* in his pants since the dawn of time.

I don't like to fuck around with Joshua's staff. It's disrespectful to him and will always lead to drama. Levi would no doubt be a good fuck, but that's all I'd want from him—to ruin him for other men. I know he would be one of those clingy guys thinking they have what it takes to keep me tied to one man. That is not something I'm entertaining right now.

The seat next to me dips as Joshua joins us, placing another round of beers on the table before slinging his arm over the back of my seat. He nods to the bar where Levi is still looking over here. "You're distracting my bartender again," he teases.

"What can I say? I'm appealing." I shrug, rolling my shoulders to ease the tension building there. It's not Levi I want. I need to get this kid out of my fucking system.

"So I wanted to talk to you about something," Joshua announces, leaning forward, arms coming to rest on the table, head slightly bowed.

I raise a brow, intrigued. Ren leans in from my other side, curiosity summoning him. "Let's say a female's kink is a role-play scene...fantasy rape," he whispers, like anyone would frown upon that shit in here. "What's the protocol for that sort of thing?"

I hold up my hand. "As long as you have consent, it's fine."

"That's not something you offer here though?" Ren clarifies, posing it as a question. If it is, it's not something we know about, and considering we're his best friends and have been coming here since the place opened, I think we'd know.

This is a personal question.

Swigging his drink, Joshua shakes his head. "No, it's not something we offer here, or something I'm looking to introduce, but I have a client who came to me asking about this stuff."

"What do you want to know, Joshua?"

"If a role-play happened as realistically as possible, can it backfire on the aggressor?"

"Get a contract in place, iron-clad—and don't do anything that's not consented in the contract," I warn him.

"So, who is it?" Ren grins, leaning more forward, like a fucking teenage girl desperate for gossip.

"Fuck off." Joshua smirks back at him. "You know I keep everything confidential."

"That's why we play here," I say, clinking his bottle with the one he brought over for me.

"Who are you going to recommend for her?" Ren pushes, knowing full well Joshua wouldn't outsource something this delicate. He's always been focused on providing a safe place for people to live out their fantasies and fetishes. Safety is a high priority for him, and role-play is where he gets his kicks.

"For fuck's sake, this guy is paranoid," Ren scoffs, getting distracted by something on his phone.

The interruption gives Joshua a reprieve. "You wanting your room tonight?" he asks, but Ren is getting agitated as fuck with whoever the hell is texting him and my interest is piqued, so I just shake my head no.

"What's going on, Ren?" I ask, picking at the label on the bottle.

Putting his phone down, he notices something across the bar and his entire demeanor changes. A smile that reaches his eyes lights up his face, and then he's standing.

"Xavi is having a meltdown or some shit. You may need to go sort his ass out. As for me, my woman just arrived. I have a night of depravity planned for her." He winks, abandoning me with yet another rescue mission.

Time to text the boy...

Pulling up at the address Xavi gave me, I find him on the curb playing with a lighter.

He looks beautiful under the hue of the moon.

Haunted.

Lost.

A shadow wanting to surrender to the night.

Getting out of the truck, I walk over to him, kicking the tip of his boot. It's then I see the burns on his hand. "Get the fuck up. We need to get that looked at before it gets infected."

Sighing, he looks up at me, narrowing those troubled brown eyes. "It'll be fine, and you're not my fucking dad," he snaps, stumbling as he tries to stand.

"You're drunk, so I'll let that slide. But I warned you about this shit before I got here, so don't try my patience, boy."

"I'm not drunk. I'm pissed off. Some prick cornered me in the bathroom." He sounds truly distressed.

My back straightens. My fists curl. "Did he fucking hurt you?"

Maybe there was more to this incident.

"What? No, he tried to kiss me," he grinds out, waltzing toward an alleyway, kicking an empty beer bottle.

I follow, making him jerk in response to my closeness.

"Why does that get you so rattled?" I ask, my tone sincere, seemingly penetrating his armor.

He turns to face me, toe to toe. When he talks, I can taste his breath. We're so close, it makes me want to inhale him.

"Because he's gay, and he thought I was too."

"And that's a bad thing?" I scoff.

"I'm not gay!" he growls, poking his finger into my chest with brass balls.

I grab his jaw and back him up against the brick wall. His pupils dilate. His breath quickens. His pink tongue swipes out to wet his lips. I lean in, pressing my hand more firmly against his jaw, relishing the moment he stiffens, but doesn't fucking fight it. His hands are by his sides, free to push me away or hit me. There's a flush to his cheeks, and I know if I rested my palm to his chest, I'd feel the rushing of his blood and pounding of his heart.

I see through his façade. I could give him what he

secretly craves right now, in this alley. Take everything from him.

"Maybe you gave him the impression you wanted to be kissed," I tell him.

"I do...I didn't...I mean, I didn't." His chest rises and falls as his eyes roam my face, dipping to my lips unabashedly.

Does he know how obvious his need is?

"And now? What if I were to kiss you? Would you want it? Or would you want to fight me? Would you fight me?"

"No."

"No to which question?" I lean in slightly so he can feel my stiff cock against his and inhale his scent, making him shiver. "No you wouldn't want it, or no you wouldn't fight it?"

It's wicked to tease his desire this way, but fuck, he makes me feel shit I shouldn't be feeling. I want to wreck him. Dismantle all this self-hate and pain and show him it's okay to be who he is. Feel what he feels. I want to draw out his pleasure by creating his pain in a way that will enlighten him, free him. Give him the pain he needs to help him heal from whatever it is that fucked his head up so bad.

"Well?"

Gulping, he asks on a shaky breath, "Are you going to kiss me?"

Fuck, I want to so bad. Instead, I rub his bottom

lip with the pad of my thumb and whisper in his ear, "You're not ready for me yet, boy. But soon."

With that, I pull away and go to my truck. It takes two minutes before the passenger door opens and he slips inside.

"Where are you taking me?"

"My place."

Flicking the light on and chucking the keys on the counter, I point to the couch. "Sit."

He doesn't argue. He looks like a wounded animal, tail between his legs as he slinks out of his leather jacket and collapses onto the seat. I grab the first aid kit and sit opposite him on the coffee table, thankful it's solid wood and can handle my weight.

"You know this is fucked up, right?" I admonish with a raised a brow, grabbing his wrist to inspect his wounds. It's just superficial and will heal.

Tipping alcohol over the sores carelessly to grab his attention makes him gasp and moan in pain. I keep eye contact with him as I do it again. This time, he exhales a shaky breath, his eyes hooded as he watches me.

"You like pain?" It's a question, but stated.

"I like to feel," he replies.

"You need an outlet for all the shit you keep bottled up inside, but burning to this degree isn't healthy," I tell him, applying cream and wrapping his hand and wrist. "There are other ways." Our eyes hold each other, communicating without words. The intensity is palpable in the air thickening around us. The room has a pulse. It's loud and undeniable.

Thud, thud, thud.

He's not going to self-destruct. I won't allow him to implode. He's going to enter my world. It's going to be a rough, a wild game of survival—of healing—of learning. I'm going to give him a fucking awakening. Change him forever...

If he makes it through it.

"What are thinking about?" he asks, desperately aching. The need in his voice nearly undoes me.

"I'm thinking Ronan is going to give you some time off and I'm going to take you somewhere for a little while."

I wait for him to pull back, to allow his mask to slip back into place, but it doesn't. Xavi is a lost boy who needs me to find him. He simply nods his confirmation. He fucking agrees and my lungs release the air I was holding. I want to strip him bare, right here and now, and show him all the ways I can make him feel better—show him he doesn't have to be afraid of who he is. No one has ever gotten under my skin quite like he does. I'm not sure if it's a weakness or a gift. But I need to get out of this room before I lose all self-control and push him too far and too quick.

"You can crash here," I tell him. "On the couch."

Marching from the room, I slam into my bedroom, the door banging off the wall. Ripping off my clothes, I go straight to the shower.

The spray is cool, but does nothing to soothe the fire raging inside me.

Resting a palm on the tile wall, I grip my hard, throbbing cock, tugging roughly. Flashes of Xa's tongue licking over his fat fucking lips makes the veins pulse and the mushroom tip bulge in anger. The ache is torturous—a beautiful fucking torture. Knowing he's in the other room is a sick kind of agony. I want nothing more than to go in there, force him to his knees, and ram my fat cock into that lush fucking mouth of his. I want him to choke on my length, stretch his lips with the girth, grab a handful of that sexy hair and wring my release into him, making him swallow every drop. Instead, I tug and pull my cock with intense ferocity, milking myself for him. I catch a glimpse of his silhouette in my peripheral, but he's gone by the time my head turns.

Ronan said he owed me, and I'm cashing in that check. I need to get away, just us two. Find out what's behind all his inner turmoil and see what the hell this thing is between us—because there's no fucking denying it. No matter how much he wants to tell himself he's not gay, he's got a hard-on for me and my cock, and I want to explore every inch of him with it.

Wrapping a towel around my waist, I poke my head into the living room and find him lying on the couch in only his jeans, the button open, and the tip of his hard cock on display, begging to be touched, licked, sucked, fucked.

Soon, boy. Soon, I'll have it all, and you'll take it all. Everything I fucking give you—until I push all your limits. We're going exploring. I'm the hunter, and you're the hunted who has nowhere left to hide.

5

Xavi

My heart is nearly beating out of my chest. It makes me wonder what the fuck I took from the bartender. The gay bartender who thought I was gay.

I'm not.

So why the fuck did I follow Blaine into his bedroom like a lovesick puppy? What was I thinking? That he was waiting for me to come to my senses so we could have sex?

A tiny thrill shoots down my spine at the image running inside my head. Naked. Sweaty. Blaine pressed against me, his mouth fused to mine. My dick is aching and hard as a rock, desperately trying to escape the confines of my jeans.

When I made it to his room, he was already in the shower. I once again misread the situation. He wasn't waiting on me. No, Blaine was taking care of things himself. I was too much of a chicken shit to stay and watch, though I wanted to. Even with the steam from the shower, I could see the curves of his broad shoulders and tapered waist. Thick, muscular thighs. Masculine as can be. And there he was, one hand pressed to the wall as he expertly jerked at his dick.

I squeeze my eyes shut, ignoring the need to touch myself.

Hard. So fucking hard.

I don't understand what's going through my head lately. With Devon, I was pissed and hated that he assumed I was gay. But with Blaine? I sort of hope he thinks I am so he'll make the first move—unbutton the rest of my jeans and take me into his hand.

My eyes pop open, and I listen in the dark. His bed creaks as he shifts, getting comfortable. The urge to get up and walk in there is maddening.

Then what?

Crawl into bed beside him and beg him to force the things on me I secretly crave?

I don't crave shit. That's the drugs.

I think. I fucking hope.

When the urge is too intense, I take matters into my own hand. I undo the remaining buttons on my jeans. Cool air kisses my hot, throbbing cock, and a bead of pre-cum dots the tip.

This is fucked up.

I'm in some cop's house about to jerk off to thoughts of him.

Under normal circumstances, this sounds like exactly the kind of shit that gets you arrested. But right now? I think I'm safe from that. Safe from the prying eyes of the world. Safe from the judgmental stares and words of people who don't understand just what the fuck is screwing with my head.

Blaine seems to see something inside me I can't see myself. And rather than exploiting it, it's as though he has a plan. I just wish I was in on said plan.

My hand wraps around my cock, making me hiss in pleasure. In the dark, with Blaine's masculine and powerful scent permeating every inch of his home, it's easy to pretend it's his hand. But his hand is bigger and stronger. I bet he'd jerk me hard. I yank to the point of pain, squeezing my eyes shut as I chase this fantasy of him.

Harder. Harder. Harder.

I'm breathing heavily, groaning quietly as my body tingles with pleasure. The need to come is overwhelming. I crave more than my hand, but it's all I have. No filthy fan girl to sink my dick into…

My dick softens slightly.

Jesus!

Blaine. Blaine. Blaine.

His growly voice. His dark, penetrating stare. His full pink lips that look like they would feel good pressed against mine. His thick cock rubbing against mine as he pins me to the wall.

Fuck!

A spurt of hot cum shoots out of me, splattering my chest. The room spins, dizzying me. Heat rushes through my veins like I've taken a hit of something super addictive—something that'll get me killed like Lex.

Goddammit, what the hell am I doing?

I peek my eyes open to inspect the mess I made. My lean, tattooed chest glistens in the moonlight. The tip of my cock still drips from my release. I'm still aroused and eager for more, despite the fact that I just whacked off like some confused freak in a cop's living room.

If we were together, would he lick the cum right off my chest?

Would he gather it with his thumb and shove it into my mouth, forcing me to taste myself?

When my dick twitches, impatient to yield to his demands, I let out a heavy sigh.

Fuck this.

Fuck Blaine.

And fuck my stupid dick.

Shame is a powerful emotion. For me, it's a muse killer and a mood destroyer. It also makes me paranoid as fuck. Ever since last night at Blaine's, I've been spinning.

I cleaned up my "mess" and snuck out of the cop's house like some sort of bad ass teenager getting away from his overbearing dad. But in my case, I was escaping my overwhelming desire to be with the cop. Whether the feeling is mutual or not is beside the point.

I don't want him.

I don't want any man.

Thank fuck I can always count on the band to remind me how to be a man. I'd woken up really fucking late this afternoon in Seth's guest bed. I don't know how the hell I got here, though my text messages leave a trail of me begging him to come get me. Now, a party is in full force downstairs. Loud as shit too.

After a quick shower where I forbade myself to think about Blaine's shower, I dress in some black, holey jeans I find in Seth's closet, one of his tight-ass white shirts, and pull back on my boots. He's such a girl, so his bathroom is stocked full of hair styling shit. Once I do a style that has my dark, overgrown hair looking messy but hot as fuck, I steal an unused toothbrush and take care of the taste in my mouth that reminds me of bad decisions from the night before.

As soon as I head downstairs, I can hear a familiar

guitar riff. Owen's showing off—alone, from the sound of it. I saunter down the stairs and scan the growing crowd. Several scantily dressed women let out squeals when they see me. I'm not an asshole, so I nod and flash them a killer smile before finding Owen.

He's sitting on the hearth of the fireplace, shirtless, a Gibson Dove acoustic in his lap and a cigarette dangling from his lips as he plays something familiar. It's not wise to try new songs with guests, so we tend to stick with what they already know. We learned that the hard way when we had an impromptu jam session one time during a party. That YouTube video still gets more "free" hits than anything we've ever produced in a studio or played onstage.

I walk over to him and fuck with his hair as he strums away on "Heartache from Below," the first power ballad we ever did.

"And then his hot best friend walks in and asks where the fucking pizza is," I croon in my voice that makes girls lose their panties in a flash. It's not the words to the song, but if you didn't know any better, you'd fall for it.

He laughs and kicks his foot out at me. I grin at him before heading into the kitchen to see what I can scrounge up. Once in Seth's massive kitchen, I find a girl sitting on the counter looking like a fucking treat.

Tiny as hell.

Long brown hair.

Fat red lips.

Her tits are spilling out of her dress, and the hem barely covers her cunt. She has short legs, but they're nice and shapely. They'd look great wrapped around me. As she types away on her phone, the glow illuminating her face, I lean against the fridge and watch her.

She's exactly what I need.

A fucking distraction.

A reminder that whatever confusing shit has been going on, is just that: confusing. I like what I see with this girl. She's my type.

My phone buzzes, and I pull it out, ignoring the missed calls from Blaine I received this morning. Flipping over to Twitter, I look to see what I'm missing out on. Lots of Owen shit—pictures of his shirtless body strumming his guitar from moments before. Even one of me messing with his hair. Fuck, these people are quick. The picture of the two of us already has over forty thousand likes. I snap a picture of the girl, a close up of just her mouth, and type: *"Where can a guy find a pretty mouth like this to kiss?"*

As soon as I submit the tweet, I watch the girl. She stares intently at the screen. Then she frowns, pulling the phone closer. When she determines it's her, her mouth parts as she mouths "Oh my God." Her blue eyes lift to mine.

"There's one," I say, like I just found the answer to my question, as I pocket my phone. "Question is, does that pretty mouth want to be kissed?"

I saunter over to her and grip both her knees, pulling her thighs apart so I can stand between them. With how short her dress is, she's probably flashing anyone in the near vicinity. I slide my hand into her hair and kiss her hard. My lips and tongue dominate hers, and she rewards me with sweet mewls.

My stomach grumbles, making her giggle.

It's enough to pull me out of the moment and remind me why I haven't eaten. I fucked up and texted Blaine to come save me last night. As a result, I slept all day trying to forget that horrible mistake.

"Come on," I growl, pulling her into my arms.

Her laughter spurs me on as I carry her through the house, past the curious onlookers, and upstairs. Once inside the guest room, I shut the door and toss her on the bed. Under her dress, I get a flash of a black thong.

"Lay back," I command. "Take off your panties and show me what I get to fuck."

She bites on her plump bottom lip and shimmies out of her thong. It gets flung at me, and then she opens her legs like a practiced whore, baring her pink pussy lips at me. This shit used to get me riled up. I can fuck for hours. I'm relentless.

So why in the ever-loving hell am I having to rub at my cock through my jeans, attempting to get it hard?

"Touch yourself," I order, buying some time. "How wet are you?"

She pushes a finger into her pussy and pulls it out. It glistens in the light. Like it's a lollipop, she sucks her finger into her mouth, making an over-the-top show of enjoying her taste.

My dick doesn't even twitch.

Not now.

Fuck.

She sits up on her knees and peels off her dress, baring her tits to me. Huge and barely staying inside her black bra. On her knees, she walks over to the edge of the bed.

"I see you looking at these," she says breathily as she squeezes her tits. "Want to fuck them?"

The idea of pressing her tits together as I fuck the cleavage is something that would normally be a no brainer.

And yet...

I need a drink or ten. I'm too sober.

Before I can state that, she's undoing my loose, borrowed jeans. They fall to my ankles unceremoniously, showing off my flaccid dick. Her look of surprise is enough to have me panicking—and panic does nothing to help the state of my dick. A thousand thoughts wash through my head about what she's thinking. It's irrational, but I can't stop the paranoia eating away at me.

"I need a drink," I rasp as I start to reach for my jeans.

"Here," she purrs, reaching for my soft cock. "Let me suck it to life."

Oh, Jesus. This is bad.

Her tongue flicks out and tastes my tip as she works my flimsy cock in her tiny hand. The more I stare in shock at my useless dick, the more terror rises up inside me. My eyes slide to her phone on the bed.

My inability to get hard could be a media fucking sensation the moment she lets go.

No. No. No.

Fucking no.

"Everything okay? I've been told I'm great at giving head."

"Yeah, I just need a minute. I just woke up." I laugh nervously.

"We can bring your friend up if you prefer? Your band mate? Owen, maybe?"

What the fuck does she mean by that? Fuck, now my dick is twitching.

"Oh…" she croons. "I think your dick likes that idea"

Fuck.

"I…uh…stop, lady."

She pouts and looks up at me in confusion. "Cassidy."

"Right…um, Cassidy. Can we take a breather for a second? I'm not feeling so hot."

"Sure," she says. "I'll just look at my phone until you're ready—"

"No!" I bark out, making her jump. "I mean…uh, please. I need to talk to my label. It's important. Can you just stay here looking so fucking pretty?"

My words make her melt.

"Lie back and make yourself feel good," I urge.

While she falls back and touches herself, I knock her phone onto the floor, yank up my jeans, and dial Ren. She's focused on getting off, so I snag up her phone and pocket it while I wait for him to answer.

No answer.

Fuck.

Reluctantly, I call Ronan. I hate having to talk to him, but desperate times call for desperate measures. I cannot have this shit getting out. This could be catastrophic to my reputation.

"Xavi Jacobs," he says in way of greeting. Cool, guarded, slightly pissed off.

"Ronan," I whisper, ducking into the adjoining bathroom. "I'm totally fucked."

"What now?" he growls.

My heart races. "I…uh, there was this girl and…" I pinch the bridge of my nose.

"Say what you have to say, man. Unless she's not breathing. In that case, don't say anything else," he says impatiently. "Out with it."

"I can't get hard."

The line goes quiet.

"Are you asking me for sex advice?"

I let out a rush of air. "Fuck no. She's saying shit about me needing Owen or one of the guys in the room to get hard. I'm afraid she's going to tell the whole fucking world. Help me. Please."

"I see. You're at Seth's from the looks of it. I'll be there in fifteen with an NDA."

Though I called him for help, I didn't expect him to be so accommodating. "Really?"

"Really. Don't say a word or do anything stupid until we talk. And, Xavi, is there anything I need to know about you and Owen?"

"What the fuck? No, of course not."

"Okay."

He hangs up, and I slink back into the bedroom as Cassidy cries out my name. She shudders on the bed. When the aftershocks subside, she grins lazily at me.

"Beautiful," I praise. "So beautiful, it makes me want to write a song."

Her blue eyes widen. "No way!"

"Get dressed and I'll play some shit for you," I say, shrugging one shoulder.

Eagerly, Cassidy throws on her clothes, then looks around for her phone.

"Private show," I say with a smile. "It's only fair since you gave me one." I give her a wink that has her sighing happily.

Luckily, since I stay here sometimes, Seth keeps an acoustic for me. It's not as nice as the one Owen's playing downstairs, but it'll do the trick. I sit on the edge of the bed and make up some chords to stall until Ronan gets here. I could probably sing about the neighbor's dog shitting on the grass and this girl would be into it based on the way she tries to sing along and sways.

Fifteen minutes on the dot, Ronan pushes into the room with a concerned Owen at his side. When Owen sees my panicked face, his eyes dart to Cassidy.

"Oh," Cassidy says, "are we, like, going to have an orgy? I'm into it, I just wasn't expecting it."

Ronan flashes her a boardroom shark smile as he pulls out a folded piece of paper from his pocket. I normally hate his stiff suit attire, but right now, he looks powerful and intimidating—which is exactly what I need from him.

"Sorry, Ms…" he trails off.

"Cassidy Holder."

Ronan pulls out a pen from his pocket and leans the paper against the wall as he scribbles something out. "This, Cassidy Holder, is a nondisclosure agreement. It's a simple document that says you are not to tell anything about what happens inside Mr. Jacobs' bedroom. Conversations, sexual activities, songs. Whatever happens is to be kept under lock and key. Are we clear?"

Her face turns red. "What's going to happen?"

Owen shoots me a confused look.

"Nothing is going to happen," Ronan assures her. "Because you're going to sign this and rejoin the party."

"But why?" she asks, her bottom lip wobbling. "What did I do wrong?"

"Nothing," I say, shooting her a firm look.

"Some people like to exploit famous people," Ronan says bluntly. "But not you, Ms. Holder."

"Never," she breathes, shaking her head.

"Then you'll be fine signing." He hands her the pen and paper. "Go on, read it. It's very clear and concise."

She takes her time reading the document, then looks up at him. "I'll be sued if I mention anything?" Her blue eyes flicker to mine, hurt shining in them. I feel like a fucking dick, but I don't want this shit out there.

"I see you understand the agreement," Ronan says.

"I guess I don't have a choice," she grumbles, scribbling her name on the line.

"You have a choice to forget this evening and enjoy the party," Ronan replies in a no-nonsense tone. "That simple."

She nods and gives me a sad look. "I still don't know what I did wrong."

"Nothing, sweetheart," Owen says, smiling. "Why don't we go back downstairs and I'll play a song for you? Your choice."

Her eyes light up. "Okay, that sounds awesome." She glances at me. "I just need my phone."

Ronan lifts a brow, silently asking if it's okay. I give him a clipped nod before handing it to her.

My mouth opens to apologize, but he shakes his head at me. Owen grabs her hand and leads her out of the room. The moment the door closes behind them, I let out a sigh of relief.

"Come here," he orders, his voice dripping with authority like Blaine's.

Heat of embarrassment or shame prickles across my skin, making me aware that I'm in the room with Blaine's best friend.

"What?" I ask, my voice husky.

"Blaine told me about last night."

My face flames, and I scowl. "I don't know what the fuck you're talking about."

Ronan approaches, his face inches from mine as he inspects me with that calculating glint in his eyes. "The part where he rescued you from yourself."

"And what else?"

His lips quirk up on one side. "There was more? He certainly didn't tell me anything else. Blaine has certain kinks, though. So there's always more with him. Don't worry," he assures me. "You don't need an NDA with him. He's a fucking vault with his boys."

His boys?

My dick—the traitorous motherfucker—wakes

up, hard and eager to be a good boy for Blaine. I've never wanted to be fucking good. What the fuck?

"I am not with Blaine," I croak out, hating how vulnerable my voice sounds.

"Oh, I know," Ronan says. "You haven't been broken in yet. Still acting out and misbehaving. If you were with Blaine, he'd sort your shit out real quick."

I want to demand he tell me how.

How will Blaine straighten me out?

Why do I want him to?

"I...I..." I trail off, grasping for an explanation.

Ronan smiles. "You need a vacation, like he says. Come on. I'll drop you by your house so you can pack a bag. Blaine's coming for you. I've been instructed to get you ready."

My head spins. "W-What? I have shit to do. You know this. I can't go on a vacation!" Not with fucking Blaine, of all people.

"I'll have Eve rearrange your schedule. Don't fight me on this. You won't win."

Evil bastard's trying to control my goddamn life.

His features soften, and he grips my shoulder. "I'm on your side, Xavi. I wish you'd get that through your thick skull."

I blink at him in confusion. We've done nothing but fight since I signed with him. I hate how much control I gave him. Creatively, schedule wise, monetarily. He'd done what he did with Cassidy and waved a contract at us. We'd been star-struck and eager. But, as time passed, I realized I wanted more wiggle room, to which he firmly told me no each time.

"I want to write some tracks to the next album. I don't want your songwriter going in and changing shit like our last album," I blurt out.

His brows furrow. "If you show me you can grow up, Xavi, I'll give you more freedom. Like any good adult role model in your life, I do things to protect you and keep the pressure off you as much as I can. Take the vacation and come back to me with something I can use. Leave the drugs and alcohol to a minimum, and maybe I'll consider renegotiating your contract."

I gape at him in shock. "Really?" Of all the times we've fought at his office over this shit...

"Give me something to work with," he says. "Now, let's get you off to Blaine."

Oh, fuck.

What did I just agree to?

I think I just sold my soul to the devil...and it's not the three-piece Armani suit wearing fucker in front of me.

The devil is a hard-bodied cop who doesn't take well to bullshit.

And now I'm going on fucking vacation with him.

Good one, Xavi. Good fucking move.

6

Blaine

Pulling down the gravel road off the beaten track toward the cabin my old man left me, I already feel ten tons lighter.

I love the city, but the shit I see with my job can leave a mark on the soul. It's good to cleanse it every once in a while. It's therapeutic being in the wilderness.

Xavi groans in his sleep, his brow furrowed from troubled dreams. I reach across the seat to rest a hand on his chest when he begins jerking a little, the visions taking hold, keeping him enslaved.

He stills beneath my touch, the lines ironing out across his forehead.

His serene innocence is now displayed on his sleeping form.

He's fucking beautiful to look at. Pale skin, a

contrast to his dark, untamed hair curling around his ears, and a straight nose leading to full lips that look firm and soft all at once.

My body aches to lean in and taste them.

In a crowded room, he can compel a sea of people with just his presence, but to be alone with him is something else entirely. When stripped of his attitude and cocksure ego, there is something vulnerable and almost delicate about him—and intensely alluring.

I raise my hand to stroke his cheek, my knuckles grazing the soft skin, causing him to stir in his sleep and become stiff beneath my touch.

His hand reaches up to grasp mine. Strong, long fingers wrapping around my fist. "What are you doing?" he asks gruffly.

Pulling my hand from his, I nod to the cabin. "We're here."

Sitting up and shifting in his seat, his brows raise and his mouth opens. "Wow, it's…"

"What?"

"Nice, big." His lips hook up briefly in a crooked grin.

"Did you think it was going to be a shack where we had to share a cot to keep warm?" I ask with a snort.

He answers my question by turning his head toward his window.

Shit, he did think that. "My grandpa built this

place with his own two hands. It's been in my family for a long time. My father passed it down to me. I like to come here to decompress," I tell him.

"And bring assholes here who need reigning in?" he remarks, rubbing his palms down his jeans anxiously.

"I've never brought anyone here." I grimace. The news seems to surprise us both.

I pull up and turn the engine off, but don't move to get out. "I don't want you to feel like this was forced on you, or that you're a prisoner here. You have to want to be here. Do you understand what I'm saying? I want to help you."

The truck falls deathly silent. My heart begins to pound while he takes his time deciding if he's ready for this.

For me.

If he wants to go back, I'll take him, but it will be hard ridding myself of the desire I have for this damn boy.

My hands tighten on the steering wheel to stop myself from grabbing him and barking, *"Tell me your ready, boy, because here I fucking come."*

"I want to be here," he finally says in a soft tone.

Opening the door, I jump out and feel an overwhelming need to smile. *He's ready.*

I'm ready. I've got a damn fever burning up inside me for this boy, and he should run because I'm going to break him to remake him. But running now won't do him any good. I'm on fire, and he's not just in my path, he's my destination.

Following me inside, he takes in the place with wide eyes and childlike awe. It's an open space including a game area with a pool table and bar, and a huge sitting area with a widescreen TV mounted above the fireplace. My favorite aspect, apart from the obvious choice, is the kitchen. It's huge with a breakfast bar doubling as an island right in the center. There's something intimate and erotic about cooking for someone else—especially if it's because you're both starving from fucking the energy out of each other all day and night.

"You want a tour?" I ask, moving toward the wooden staircase at the back of the cabin.

Shrugging out of his jacket, he runs his fingers through his hair before shoving them in his jeans pockets and nodding. "Sure."

I can sense his nervous energy. It riles up the beast inside.

Gesturing to the first door when we reach the top, I say, "Towels and spare linens." Without losing pace, I open the door and step inside. "Master room."

I watch as his eyes take in the space, widening as he scans the sexual pleasure apparatus placed beside the king-sized bed in the middle of the room. I had it set up for pleasure, but never found anyone I wanted to bring here. *Until now.*

"Is that a shower?" he asks, making me grin. Of all the things to ask about...

"It is."

The entire back wall is a glass-sliding panel leading to a shower the full width of the room. I follow him as he surveys the outer wall also being made from glass looking out into the surrounding forest. I had it installed last summer. Something about seeing and being seen makes my cock throb. "You want to try it out?" I tease.

"So you can watch? Perv," he scoffs.

"Scared it will make you gay?" I mock, chuckling when he narrows his eyes on me.

"Fuck you," he spits, an ugly, defensive demeanor taking over.

Maybe it's because we're here in my space, or perhaps it's the fact that I'm done with his fucking mouth being used to abuse instead of amuse me, but my hand snaps out, backhanding him across the cheek, my knuckle catching his lip. He rocks backward, falling against the wall and gasping in shock.

"You fucking hit me!"

I close in on him, drowning him in my height and weight. Grasping his jaw between my thumb and forefinger, I tip his gaze up to mine. "I've let that line pass your lips one too many times, and you seem to think it's acceptable to say it but not do it," I growl, leaning down to lick at the spot of blood blooming on his bottom lip.

He flinches at first, then relaxes beneath me. I take it a step further, finally giving in to the need to feel his lips on mine. I nip his fat, pouty lip while keeping eye contact.

An exhale shivers past his lips. I'm not sure if it's panic or excitement, but I take it as the latter and swipe my tongue against the seal of his mouth, testing him. When it parts, I plow inside to caress his tongue. Peppermint and cigarettes attack my taste buds. Warm, wet flicks of his tongue drive me fucking crazy.

Come out of your shell, little boy. See what's out here. Show me you're a man.

The kiss is slow, exploring, as he traces the recesses of my mouth.

I offer persuasive encouragement, groaning with pleasure, dancing my tongue against his. It soon becomes hungry, our mouths dueling, caressing with urgency, ravishing each other. I pull back, breathless and ready to fuck him raw. His eyes are expressive and shine bright with lust. The furrow of his brow tells me he's fighting with himself, wanting this, but scared to admit it to himself.

Keeping myself from being reckless with him, I trace the outline of his mouth with my fingertip. "Why are you so afraid to feel what you do?" I implore, desperate for all his secrets, his words, truths, confessions.

"I don't know how to turn it off."

"Turn what off?"

His bottom lip quivers, emotion consuming him. I grasp his face, stroking the pads of my thumbs over his cheeks, my eyes begging him to open up to me.

"The pain, fear, truth of what I think I may be," he rushes out.

It's painful to see him so troubled. Being this invested is new to me, and it's dangerous because I'm going to love it even more when he finally accepts what he's feeling—when I get to be inside him, mind, body and fucking soul. He's got me all caught up in him, snared by his achingly defined beauty and tortured soul—the desperate need he has to be rescued. That's what I fucking do.

He was meant for me.

And here I am, boy.

"You can be free here. It's just you and me." I touch my lips to his before pulling away. "Take a shower. It was a long drive," I urge him, leaving the room so he can regain his composure.

I retrieve our bags from the truck, grab wood from a stack I left here last time to start a fire, and load the kitchen with the groceries before I even hear the shower blast from above. I snag our suitcases and head upstairs, dropping his in one of the spare rooms. He's going to want space.

Going into my room, I find a pile of his discarded clothes left at the shower entrance.

The spray hums, pitter-pattering against the glass wall, steam distorting the top of the glass, but not hiding his form from me. I see him fully beneath the spray.

His stance emphasizes the lean muscle of his thighs and ass, tapering off to a slim waist and structured back. His head is bowed as if in worship.

Worship me, boy.

Creamy, flawless skin beckons me to blemish it.

Soon.

His physique is athletic and undeniably fucking delicious. I want to devour every inch of him until he's a quaking mess of sweat and cum.

Swiping the water from his face, he turns toward the glass, our gaze's clashing. He freezes, fists tightening beside him, jaw ticking, dick stiffening to a salute. I stride over to the divide between us and rest my palms on the see-through barrier. Licking my lips, I groan, my mouth filling with saliva. "Touch your cock for me, boy. Show me how you punish yourself for feeling shit you think you shouldn't," I tell him.

He falters, his shoulders collapsing and eyes closing, but the steady rise and fall of his chest betrays him. He's so fucking turned on, his dick looks harder than granite.

The veiny, thick length must be a good eight inches and pulsing with an ache I know too well. The tip is glistening like a juicy fucking treat begging to be engulfed by my throat.

The prolonged anticipation nearly has me smashing the glass and taking his ass roughly against the outer wall. But then his eyes open, flaring with a newfound light. Confidence and sureness he hasn't displayed up until this point.

He grasps his cock firmly in his palm and strokes, slow and tortuous. "Are you just going to watch?" he asks, muffled by the sound of pouring water behind him.

"It's only fair," I say with a smirk. "You've seen me. Now, it's my turn."

Reaching out, he pins his hand where mine lay on the other side of the divider. Our eyes meet, and we stare at each other as he tugs and pulls on his dick, his thumb caressing the tip, rubbing in the juices leaking there. My cock strains against the zipper of my jeans, screaming at me to take it out and mimic the boy's movements.

His fingers stroke and dance over his cock, working himself like he's making a dark, edgy, euphoric riff.

His lips part as he pants and moans. Quickening his pace, he cocoons the girth in his fist, jerking with ferocity, up and down, squeezing, rubbing, embracing. His face contorts almost in agony. His moans bounce around the shower as white ribbons of cum spurt against the window, his bulging mushroom head pulsating his release all for me.

I want to lick the salty seed and fuck his face with his load all over my tongue.

He sucks at the air to fill his spent lungs, his dick softening but not going completely flaccid, then releases his dick like it's on fire. Stepping into the spray, he turns his back to me, shame coating him more than the water.

I'm going fucking burst a vein if I don't take care of my own raging hard cock, but he needs to know what he just did is okay.

He's fucking safe with me.

I strip out of my clothes and slide open the door, stepping inside. The water dampens my skin in its warmth, doing nothing to cool my heated flesh.

"What are you doing?" he balks, fear glimmering in his eyes.

"Taking a shower," I reply, ignoring him and going about washing myself, trying not to relieve the ache down below.

"Do people know about you?" he asks after a moment of nothing but the splashing of water.

"Know what?" I turn to face him.

His eyes dance over my body, lowering to my cock and back up to my eyes. "That you're into guys?"

"If you're asking if I hide who I am, the answer is no. I am who I am. I'm not ashamed of my sexual preference. It doesn't define me in any other aspect of my life. It's not a choice I made. It's not something we can control. It's a part of who we are, not all we are."

"So, who are you?" he asks with a sense of urgency.

I ponder his question for a moment. "I'm a detective, a good friend, loving son. A compassionate, loyal, happy, and slightly depraved, gay man." I take a step closer. "Who are you?"

"I don't know," he chokes, his eyes holding mine, sending my heart pounding. "What's it like?"

"What's what like?" I ask, gruffness making my voice sound like a growl.

He swallows, and I watch the movement of his throat. "Being with a man?"

The water showers down around him, providing him a sense of shelter, obscurity.

"It's freeing." My attention darts to his full, pink lips. "When it's something you want, crave—when it's a strong desire gnawing away at you, begging for release, relief, permission, it can be everything."

"I don't want it. I fucking hate that I even think about you," he snarls, desperate to convince himself more than me.

Fucker.

I step toward him and clench his balls in my fist, making him holler and grab my arm.

"What the fuck! Let go," he cries out, panic in his expression.

"*You* let go. Fucking drop your hands now," I order, squeezing his balls, making his torso tense, the lean muscle contracting.

His hands drop, and his breathing increases in massive swallows.

"Apologize for being a little brat," I demand.

When he doesn't respond, I tighten my hold. I use my other hand to grip his throat, dragging his head toward me. "Your cock is thickening with every passing second I hold your balls at ransom, boy. Your lips are aching to be kissed again, and your ass is twitching with anticipation of when I'm going to sink my big, fat cock inside it—to the hilt. I'll have you coming in seconds with my hand, my tongue, and my dick. And you won't hate it. You'll fucking love it." I tease his lips with a swipe of mine. "Now, tell me you're sorry and I'll let you touch my cock."

The tip of his dick pokes into my thigh, his labored breathing almost out of control.

"I'm sorry, I'm so fucking sorry," he blurts out. And he is. His brows are furrowed and all confidence is gone. He wants acceptance and approval.

This is a reward I can give.

I kiss the tip of his nose. "Good boy. Now, wrap your hand around my cock and play me like you played yourself earlier. When I come, I'll release your balls."

His touch is soft at first, unsure and sloppy, but when I tighten my hold on his throat, his hand grips my cock more firmly, stroking the length. Dark orbs search mine, pupils dilated to pinpricks, a glaze of yearning shimmering. The water turns cool, saturating our fevered flesh. I want to lick all the beaded drops from his skin.

Feeling his palm on my cock is driving me insane. My composure is slipping. All I want to do is hurt and fuck him.

Working my cock like it's his own, he massages my length, giving the tip attention until my balls draw tight and warmth unfurls up my spine. Then I'm fucking coming, hot, furious, and all over us both. The creamy fluid decorates his torso and my forearm. I groan and shudder as the remaining wave of pleasure ripples through my cock.

Releasing my grip on his balls, but not his throat, I swipe my finger through the cum before the water washes it away and bring it to my lips, tasting myself, then crashing my lips to his, forcing my way into his waiting mouth. I ravish him, and he fucking takes everything I have to give him. Then, I release him.

"Thank you. Now, thank me," I demand.

"Thank you," he says, his voice quivering and body shaking from the cold water now beating down on us.

I switch off the shower and grab us each a towel. "Get dry, then come down for some food. I put your bag in the guest room down the hall," I tell him as I make my way to the closet for some fresh clothes.

"Does that make me gay now?" he calls across the room.

A sigh rattles my chest. "Xavi, you don't need to label things, especially when it makes you so on edge. Do you want to tell me why you're so afraid of being gay or people thinking you are?"

No.

He's going to hold onto that shit until I force it out of him.

And I will.

"I want to sleep. Can I just be alone for a while?" He frowns, rubbing his hand over the sores on his wrist.

"Sure. I'll keep something in the microwave for you in case you wake up and get hungry."

"Okay, thank you."

I watch him leave the room, head bowed and shoulders slumped. I don't know whether we've taken a step forward or two steps back.

Either way, he's stuck here with me, and we're not leaving until we make headway.

7

Xavi

Holy shit.

What have I done?

I knew this would happen...*us*. At least to a certain degree. Hell, I agreed to it. Now, though, I'm rethinking my reasoning.

If this gets out...

The urge to check social media is more addictive than any drug I've ever consumed. I throw on some sweatpants after my shower and hunt down my phone. When I swipe to turn it on, I'm irritated to discover I have zero bars of service.

What. The. Hell.

We're in butt fucking Egypt, so of course we don't have signal.

My hand trembles as I set the phone down on the dresser and stare at it. What do I do? I told Blaine

I wanted to sleep, but my mind is buzzing. I need a smoke, but I don't think he'll like it if I light up in his house. I grab a pack of smokes and my Zippo, and pocket them before throwing on a shirt. I'm not eager to face off with him right now, so I sneak through the modernized cabin on a trek for the outdoors.

The heat of his stare burns into me as he cooks in the kitchen, but I ignore it. My stomach grumbles the moment I inhale something savory. I'm too jittery to eat, though.

As I step outside, the chill of the evening air nips the exposed flesh of my arms and bare feet. I relish the sting. There's a swing on the darkened porch, so I plop down on it, propping my feet up on a table in front of it. I fish out my smokes and light the end before sucking down a drag, trying and failing to get my body to stop shaking.

I jacked off in front of him.

And then…

Fuck. I'm so fucked.

Ignoring the stiffening of my dick at the memory of how it felt to hold Blaine's cock in my grip, I take another drag. I blow out the calming air harshly and study my Zippo in the moonlight.

If Lex were here, I'd demand he fix what's wrong with me. Because he saw it even when I couldn't. And he loved me anyway. He was awesome like that. Not judgmental. Wise. Always straight to the point. My throat aches with emotion. He was too fucking young to die.

Tears prickle at my eyes, and I fucking hate it. I hate how fragmented my mind feels all the damn time. I just need...I need a reprieve, goddammit.

I need a reprieve from me.

"I need a reprieve from me," I croon, my voice husky from emotion. I like the way the words sound. Raw and brittle. It'd make a good hook.

The crickets are chirping in a relaxing cadence that chills my nerves a bit. I think about more lyrics that could work while tapping my Zippo on the wood of the swing for the beat. My mind drifts back to Lex.

What would he think about Blaine?

He'd probably be jealous at first, then laugh and give me shit. Me with a cop is fucking insane enough as it is. But Lex would want me to be happy, no matter if it was with a man or a woman. I know this deep down. Yeah, Lex would smile, his whole soul shining, and say, "You do you, brother."

But I don't even know who I am. I don't even know who I want to be.

Lex's laughter echoes in my head, and I tremble. I press my cigarette between my lips and flip open the Zippo. The flame dances in the darkness, enticing and alluring. I run it across my forearm, hissing at the sting. When I can't take the burn any longer, I flip the lid closed and exhale the plume of smoke. I finish my cigarette before tossing it to the porch floor and stubbing it out with my bare foot.

"I don't even know who I am," I sing, my voice low and sad. "I don't even know who I want to be." I scrub at my face, fighting the confusion warring within me. "I need a reprieve from me."

"New song?"

I jerk at the sound of Blaine's deep voice. "Maybe."

"I like it." He steps over to me and hands me my acoustic. "Heard you singing and thought this might help. Dinner is in the oven."

"Thanks," I mutter as I set it on the table. I close my eyes, hoping he'll leave me alone.

"What the hell, Xa?"

Pain lances through my arm as he grips it, his features dark and menacing in the shadows.

"What?" I growl.

"You need to quit this shit," he bites out, releasing my arm. "It's fucked up."

"Whatever, man."

He squats down in front of me so we're eye to eye. "In my house, have some respect, boy."

I tense at the husky way he calls me "boy." Every time he says it, heat burns up my spine.

"I like the pain of it," I tell him, meeting his glare with one of my own.

"As long as you're here, you're not doing that shit," he says, nodding to my Zippo.

I ignore him until he stands and starts to walk away.

"Why won't you let me burn?" My words are whispered, mostly to myself. Maybe they're lyrics, maybe they're a plea.

He walks back over to me and sits down. His fingers dig into my jaw as he turns me to look at him. My body tingles from his touch.

"You like pain?" he asks, a challenge in his tone.

Of course I rise to the occasion. "Yeah, you got a problem with that?"

His lips curl into a sinister smile that makes my stomach clench in anticipation. "I've got a problem that you're inflicting the pain yourself. That's my job, boy."

"You want to hurt me?"

"Among other things."

"Why?"

"Because I like it. And based on your need to feel as a distraction from what's going on inside you, I'd say you'll like it too."

"Like spank me?"

At this, he laughs. The sound is rich, deep, and vibrant. I decide right then, I really fucking love his laugh. Reminds me of the way Lex and I would laugh until we cried. My bandmates and I are close, but I've never been as close to them as I was with Lex. The thought of laughing without a care in the world like so many days in my past has a trickle of hope flickering inside me.

"Spanking is for the Christian Greys of the world," he says, smirking.

"Like the dude from that porn movie?"

"I know you're not sheltered, boy. That was far from fucking porn. Mr. Grey is refined and structured. Contracts and bullshit." He lifts a brow as he drags his stare down to my split lip. "I'm more of an animal. Feral and possessive. The need to dominate. Control is threaded into my DNA. Every breath, every thought, every action is fueled by my desire to hunt my prey. It's what drove me to join the police force."

"So, spanking's out," I say tightly.

He rubs his thumb along my jaw, making my hairs stand on end. "I'm not limited on my ways of punishing. If I need to whip my boy into shape and the only thing I have available is my hand, then I'll use my damn hand."

I'm not sure how I feel about getting spanked.

My dick's semi-hard in my sweats, though.

"What are you so afraid of?" he asks, his palm sliding down my throat. He squeezes slightly. "Tell me—and don't fucking lie."

I swallow and close my eyes. "I don't know."

"You want to burn so goddamn badly?" he asks, his voice a deep growl.

I snap open my eyes. "Yeah."

"Then I'm going to let you burn." He leans forward and kisses my lips chastely. "But I'm going to be the one to burn you." His teeth tug at my bottom lip, sending curls of pleasure dancing down to my dick. "Not just on your arms." He releases my neck and drags his knuckle down the side of my throat. "Here," he says as he circles my nipple over my shirt, "and here."

My breath hitches when he teases my other nipple. Burning my nipples sounds like fucking torture. So why the hell am I turned on?

"And here," he murmurs, running his knuckle over my lower abs.

I nearly stop breathing as I anticipate him going lower, but instead, he runs his knuckle over my inner thigh.

"Maybe here too. I haven't decided." He sounds amused. "I'm going to make you cry."

I scoff. "Fucking right."

"Sorry to break it to you, Xa, but you don't know shit."

Scowling, I shove his hand away. "And you don't know shit about me."

"You're transparent as hell," he says, unaffected by my pissy attitude. "You hide from your feelings until they eat you alive. And rather than letting *them* consume you, *I'm* going to be the one consuming." He leans forward, his mouth at my ear, tickling me. "I am ravenous, boy. Fucking starved for you."

I let out a surprised groan when he nips at my earlobe.

"Finish working on your song. I'm going to plate up some food." He stands, abandoning me on the swing with a half hard dick and whole heart bursting with confusing feelings.

Burn...burn...burn...

I want you to hurt me.

The song unravels inside my head. I snag up my guitar, eager to put music to the words. With my eyes closed, I strum the chords and sing along.

I'm lost in thought when the swing moves as he sits back down. I'm not sure how much time has passed, but he's set out two plates and a couple beers. I set my guitar down on the ground and pick up my plate.

"This doesn't smell like a frozen lasagna," I say as I stab at the steaming food with my fork. I groan as I take a bite. "This is too fucking good to be frozen."

He chuckles. "While your lazy ass was sleeping in the truck, I ran into the store to get a few necessities. A lady named Hilda always has something home cooked, ready for reheat. Lasagna is a town fave."

"I love Hilda," I say as I inhale the lasagna.

"She's barely five feet tall and has a wart on her face. Still love her?"

"Yes," I joke. "I'm going to have all her babies."

"You can tell her next time we run into town."

We finish our food as he tells me about some of the rookie cops he works with. I'm enjoying his stories while drinking a beer…until I realize how domestic this all feels. Familiar—like with Lex—and easy.

I jump to my feet, suddenly alive with nerves. "I need to go to bed." Before he can argue, I snag my guitar and haul ass upstairs.

It felt like a fucking date just now.

A date I was enjoying.

I'm torn between wanting to throw a goddamn tantrum and running back downstairs to keep the night going. Instead, I pace the bedroom floor.

Back and forth.

Back and forth.

Back and forth.

I stare at my Zippo I threw on the bed. The urge to flip it open and scald my skin is intense. I could. But Blaine said…

He wants to hurt me.

A calm washes over me at the thought of giving my pain over for him to control. I'm always so mentally fucking exhausted, a weight lifts at the thought.

Before I change my mind, I storm out of the room on a hunt for him. I find him in the kitchen washing the few dishes we dirtied up. When he sees my manic expression, his features harden.

"When shit piles up so high in my head, the only way for me to make it go away is to burn it.

Something about that flame against my skin, it leaves me blank and unfeeling inside. And when you…" I run my fingers through my messy hair, tugging to the point of pain. "You cause all these confusing feelings to worsen. I feel like my head is going to explode."

"But…" he trails off, challenging me to fucking beg for what I need.

"But I need you to do it for me. You said you would, and I fucking need it. Right now."

"You want me to hurt you, yes?"

I swallow and nod.

"Say the words, boy." He stalks over to me, until we're nose to nose. "Say them."

"I can't," I whisper, my cock achingly hard between us.

He grips my hips and pushes me against the wall. I let out a hiss when he rocks his hips against mine, allowing me to feel how aroused he is too. His lips fuse to mine, and I let out a defeated groan as he dominates me with his kiss. He fists his hand in my shirt and pulls me even closer.

"Say it, Xa." He kisses me so deep, it makes me dizzy. "I need to hear you say them. *You* need to hear you say them."

My body aches and buzzes with the need to feel the burn he promised he'd deliver—a pain that will numb my thoughts and calm my tumultuous heart.

"Please, Blaine," I mutter. "Hurt me."

He smiles against my lips. "Good boy."

Those words are a shot of heroin straight into my veins. I love the way they feel sliding through me, making me high.

Blaine's good boy.

Fuck.

I want to do this...whatever *this* is.

Holy shit.

This is happening.

I'm in the middle of Blaine's room, my hands raised above my head, and cuffed to a metal rack in the ceiling. He made me remove my T-shirt, but keep my pants on, which, for reasons I hate myself for, disappointed me.

I fucking love having his eyes on my junk. It makes me painfully hard. I love the ache he evokes within me—the burn.

Burn...burn...burn...

He takes my lighter from my pocket and lights a small red candle he pulled from a drawer. My eyes track his movements, anticipation thickening the air around us. The glow of the flame flickers its promise.

"When I first saw you, my dick throbbed with the images I conjured up in my mind of you strung up just like this," he croons, his eyes darkening like a predator about to pounce. "When I came to your house the night you got into a fight, I had to battle all my instincts not to give you a whipping, then spread you out over the couch, rip those tight wet jeans from your body, and spread your ass cheeks before filling you up with my big, fat cock. Pushing past the muscle, skin on skin, until you cried out in pain, then pleasure."

He moves closer, and the blood rushes through my veins, pounding my heart like a drum inside my chest. "That smirk you do so effortlessly should be a crime. It's maddening not to be able to kiss it from your lips. I want to feel your lips around my cock, pump my release down your throat, taste myself on your tongue for days," he taunts. I gulp and shift my feet, trying to hide my raging hard-on, but he knows—he fucking knows what I like more than I do.

Lifting the candle high over my shoulder, he allows the wax to pour from the top onto my skin and watches my face for a reaction.

A hiss leaves my lips as it makes contact, the sting like tiny needles poking into my flesh. The smile from his lips makes my insides dance. He enjoys this—me—hurting me. Pleased with my reaction, he lowers his arm, making the contact of wax to my skin swifter. The drips run a couple inches down my pectoral muscle before solidifying, the red stripes like art against my pale flesh.

I focus on the pain. It's the only thing that's real to me. The sweet release allows all the murky, dirty guilt inside me to leak free, pouring out the toxic hate I hold for myself. When his hand swipes away the wax and his wet tongue kisses over the sting, I groan. The pain and pleasure is mind-altering. I want to chase the high it gives me. No drugs can give me this.

The familiar burn ignites my flesh as the wax drips on my chest. My cock strains and my breathing quickens with every single drop. The fire ebbs, then a new fire begins inside me as his lips stroke over my nipples, teasing, tempting, promising. I want to scream for him to touch my cock. *Please fucking touch me everywhere and give me everything I've denied myself.* But I'm too fucking cowardly to ask, to admit it's what I want. It only makes me crave the pain.

"Hurt me," I choke out, desperate to be punished.

Lex's sad eyes flash behind my eyelids. I want to reverse time and tell him everything I should have before he died.

It was real, Lex. I wish I could have admitted that. Maybe things could have ended differently...

When the heat stops, I open my eyes to find Blaine standing before me, harnessing a fucking whip, like some sexy modern-day cowboy.

"I'm going to lash you ten times, and if you don't beg me to stop, I'll reward you." He strides around me so he's at my back. Large, warm hands touch the waistband of my sweatpants, heat from his body being so close mists over my back, his breath just above my ear. "You won't be needing these," he hums, pushing them down my legs.

My cock springs up, slapping my lower stomach, and my ass cheeks contract. It's exhilarating having him behind me. It heightens everything. When you don't know what's coming, it's electrifying. A chill races up my spine as he steps back. I fist the restraints, preparing myself for the crack of the whip.

The hiss through the air is my only warning before a slash of hellfire explodes across my back. I balk, jerking forward from the contact, then almost whimper from the thrill of it. The sting rages, and my cock throbs. Pleasure ripples through me when the next one hits.

The hurt is too fucking good.

"Two," Blaine barks from behind me, his voice gruff with need.

The next one whips out, finding purchase across my ass cheeks.

Crack, whoosh, snap.

Fire.

Pain.

Pleasure.

Burn…burn…burn.

Five…

Fire.

Pain.

Pleasure.

Burn...burn...burn.

Six... seven...eight...nine...

My body sags when the last one hits, the euphoria sending shockwaves of adrenaline through my system. My chest heaves with exhausted, lust-filled breaths.

"You're such a good boy, Xavi. Fucking perfect," Blaine growls, sweat beading on his bare chest, his cock straining the zipper of his jeans. Is he going to fuck me with that now? My thoughts wander as he drops the whip and bends to his knees in front of me.

Fuck.

Grabbing my hips, he smiles up at me before his tongue swipes out to taste the salty goodness glistening the head of my dick. My dick twitches from the contact, and heat warms my spine. Holy shit, this cop is licking my dick.

"I want to fucking drain your cock, boy. Take everything you have left to give. Tell me what you want me to do," he demands.

I answer like the good boy I am. "I want you to suck my dick." I don't feel the usual wash of guilt, humiliation. No, I fucking earned the pleasure by enduring the pain.

"Good boy," Blaine tells me, and I blossom under his praise like he's the sun and I'm a flower desperate not to wilt away.

When his mouth opens to take me in, I hold my breath. The warmth of his lips as they descend my length is better than anything I've ever felt. My entire body tingles with sensation, hyperaware of all contact. His hot tongue slips over my cock, slurping away. His head bobs up and down the length, taking me down his throat. My knees buckle, and my balls draw up. I bite my lip so I don't blow too fast. I want to relish this, live in the moment of it as long as possible.

He sucks me hard and deep, hollowing out his cheeks. Spit drools all over me, lubing my dick, creating a slip and slide of gratification. Kisses trace down my dick to my balls. He sucks them into his mouth and hums around them. It almost makes me cry out from the agony of the pleasure. He's an artist down there. We fit together perfectly, lock and key. A closed fist grips the base of my dick while his lips go to work on the bulging head, sucking, slurping, licking, flicking, tugging, up and down my shaft. When I can't take anymore, I lose it and buck my hips forward, fucking his face, and he lets me. His fingers grip my sore ass cheeks as he punishes his throat by forcing me harder and deeper. I cry out, and my spunk spurts in scorching waves, splashing the back of this throat. He laps me up, taking every drop. My body shudders from the force of the emotional release. A tear leaks from my eye.

That was everything.

Getting to his feet, he swipes the tear with his thumb and grasps my chin, forcing our eyes to clash. "You're beautiful, boy. You taste like pain and glory, and I can't get enough." Leaning forward, he licks my lip, then sucks it into his mouth. My flavor is still potent on his tongue.

Show me.

See me.

Please me.

Burn…burn…burn…

8

Blaine

Laying in my bed with Xavi sprawled out next to me on his stomach, naked and sated, is rewarding. I knew he needed me, just didn't know how badly that need was.

After applying some balm to his back, he collapsed on the bed and hasn't moved since. His breathing is labored, but I know he's awake.

"Tell me what you're thinking about when you use the lighter on yourself," I say, staring up at the ceiling.

Silence fills the room as he sucks in his breath and holds it. "The world around me crumbled when Lex died. I let him down, and the guilt fucking eats away at me." Honesty makes his words raw and ragged.

"So the burn is to punish yourself?"

"It was at first, and now it's a need—a craving to escape my head."

Leaning up on my elbow, I turn to face him, stroking over his shoulder in a soft caress.

"How did he die?"

"Overdose." His voice thickens with emotion.

"He was gay, right?"

He turns sharply, his brow crashing. "How would you know that?"

"I'm a detective. It was a hunch."

His head drops back onto the pillow as he faces me, shifting his body to get comfortable. "Lex had this energy, you know? He could walk in a room, and immediately, it was a party, a better place to be. His laughter was contagious. He infected everyone he came into contact with." A smile dances on his lips. "The night he died..." he swallows hard, "we spoke about his feelings for me." Tears build in his dark eyes. I want so bad to catch it, kiss it away, but I don't move. I allow him to finally release what's inside him. "I fucking felt it too, you know? But I was so scared, so terrified of what it meant about me. His brother, Owen? He was always talking about marketability and how our image is what sold us. Four single guys was sellable to our female fans. I felt the pressure to be something I wasn't. Owen needed me to be this perfect front man—straight and a pussy magnet." Squeezing his eyes closed, he chokes. "I told Lex I wasn't gay. That I was flattered, but we were just friends and would only ever be friends. Just fucking friends." Water drips from his eyes, scorching a path over his nose and seeping into the pillow. "I made him feel like shit, made him want that hit."

"No, don't do that. He was an addict. He injected that shit into himself."

"But if I was honest with him," he whispers. "If I'd told him it was real… Blaine, it was real, and I lied to him."

"Then what? His addiction would have disappeared? Whatever happened, he was still going to inject that poison into his veins that night, Xavi."

He nods, the movements stiff and his jaw tense. "Deep down, I know that. But he still died with my lie in his mind."

"You weren't ready, and he probably knew that. You were best friends. He knew you, Xa—he fucking knew you." I pull him into my arms, letting him release all his anger and tears. "It's going to be okay, boy. I promise."

I need a reprieve from me.

I don't even know who I am. I don't even know who I want to be.

I need a reprieve from me.

I like the pain. I fucking need it.

To feel the flame, suppress the blame.
I need a reprieve from me.

Why won't you let me burn?
Show me how. Make me learn.

Burn...burn...burn...
I need a reprieve from me.
Show me how. Make me learn.

Burn...burn...burn...

I don't want to feel anymore. Everything's too raw.
Pain and sorrow are too hard to swallow.
I need a reprieve from me.
I'm already burning.
Ignite my yearning.

Burn...burn...burn...

Show me.
See me.
Please me.

Burn...burn...burn...

Hurt me.

I reread the lyrics he eloquently wrote in his open notebook, and a heavy sigh leaves my lips. We've been at the cabin for two weeks now, and I expected him to go stir fucking crazy with no Internet or parties to act foolish at, but he's surprised me. Writing new lyrics every day, strumming new melodies. It's incredible to watch his process, to see the magic come together before my very eyes. He appears to have reclaimed himself while being out here.

Opening up sexually has lifted an enormous weight from him, but it worries me that in a week we will be back in the city and the pressure will be back on him. A knot forms in my gut at the idea of not having him in my bed. Ever since the night of his first whipping, he's spent every night in my bed, sleeping and touching, but not fucking. That's new for me— the buildup, the intimacy—and I don't want to let go of it. He will be going back to his own soon enough, and that leaves a chill around my heart.

I didn't expect to be this invested, this connected to someone. But it's undeniable, the affection I have for the boy. A week left of having him to myself. Then back to reality. Back to our lives. Back to the pressure of being this pussy-eating rock god.

He stirs in his sleep, the dark curls of his hair falling over his eyes as he shifts onto his side. "You been watching me long, perv?" He grins, and I want to tongue fuck the dimple it creates.

"Long enough to want to eat you, boy," I tease, lurching forward and yanking at his jeans. He thrashes and pretends to try to flee, but he soon begins laughing hard, making my dick twitch.

I yank his jeans down and groan at the sight of his bare ass, then sink my teeth into the flesh on display for me. He yelps from the puncture, then pushes his hips up, presenting himself to me.

My rough palms splay his cheeks so my tongue can flick out to rim the crease. His face burrows into the cushions as I rim his knot, devouring him, dribbling my saliva over him so I can push a finger inside his ass while I massage his asshole with my tongue.

Moans hum through the room.

My cock is hard and ready, but he's not. I have yet to fuck him like I want to.

I plow my finger into him and curl my arm around his waist, grasping his cock in my palm and squeezing. Dragging my fist up his shaft, I kiss and caress his ring while finger fucking his hole fast and hard, adding another digit when he cries out in pleasure.

Cum drips down my fist as he shudders his release—hot, intense, fast.

Grabbing my own cock, I rub it up and down his flesh, pushing his cheeks together and cocooning my cock as I pump my hips forward, letting his ass crack jerk me off.

When he looks over his shoulder at me, I lose my

load all up his back. I fucking want inside him so bad, it's torture.

"You ever going to fuck me, perv?" he asks with a raised brow.

I stiffen everywhere and count down inside my mind to calm myself and prevent from wrecking his tight little hole in one thrust. Once I have myself under control, I lick my lips. Bending down, I kiss his asshole. "Soon, when you're ready for me, boy."

But the truth is, I'm not sure I'm ready.

The moment I truly have him, I'm afraid I may never let him go.

That's scary as hell for a guy like me—one who likes to dabble and play, but never stays. This broken, tortured boy, though...

Fuck, he makes me want things I've never wanted before.

More.

"What is this place?" Xavi asks, hiding a smile.

"A honky tonk bar. Ever heard of one?"

His nostrils flare, and his eyes light up with amusement. "I sing rock, not country, man. This is the kind of shit they sing about in songs. Never thought it was real life."

"It's real," I say with a chuckle.

He picks up his beer and sips on it while my eyes track the other patrons. We've been cooped up in the cabin and I thought we were due for a night out. Problem with Xavi is he's fucking famous. You can't go in public without people noticing him.

Unless you go to the most redneck bar you can find.

And make him wear a ball cap.

My eyes land on his, and I admire how fucking hot he is wearing my Yankees ball cap. The bill shadows his face and highlights his pouty mouth. I've been hard ever since we sat down at this high-top table. I want his mouth on mine, then wrapped around my dick.

"You have a possessive glint in your eyes," he says, biting the inside corner of his bottom lip. "You can't suck my cock in front of everyone. They'll kick our asses."

Leaning forward, I stretch my leg between his under the table. "I was thinking your lips on my dick sounded better."

He tenses and darts a nervous glance over his shoulder. As much as I want to flaunt Xavi Jacobs as my boy, he's not ready for that. Not even fucking close.

"Later," I promise. "Maybe even in the parking lot if you're a good boy."

His Adam's apple bobs and he lets out a chuckle.

"And if some cowboys walk by? Then what? This doesn't seem like the kind of town that accepts..." he trails off and frowns.

Fuck, those lips are going to be the death of me.

"Accepts what?" I demand, rubbing at his leg with mine.

His cheeks blaze crimson, and he dips his head, hiding his features. Reaching forward, I put a finger under his chin and lift his gaze to meet mine. I arch a brow, challenging him.

"Whatever this is," he grinds out, his jaw clenching.

"Right now, it's called fucking around." I wink at him. "Soon, it'll be just plain ol' fucking."

His full lips tug into a smile. I pull away when a waitress with big tits brings us another round of beers.

"Doll, I've been looking at you for an hour now trying to place where I know you," she says, tapping her cheek as she attempts to remember. "Did you go out with Lucy Monroe from Madison High a few years ago?"

"Nah," he says. "I'm not from around here."

"I swear I know you," she whines.

"Can you bring us some potato skins?" I ask, changing the subject. "Extra sour cream?"

"Oh, sure, handsome. I'll get right on it," she purrs, stroking my bicep. "Holler if you need anything."

She bounces off, and Xavi lets out a heavy sigh.

"She likes you," he says, his eyes dark with irritation.

"Does that bother you?"

"I didn't think it would, but I didn't like her touching you."

"Because I'm yours?" I challenge.

His smile is so fucking hot. "Something like that."

"I'm going to reward that sexy mouth later. Jealousy looks really good on you."

He darts his gaze over to where the waitress is talking to another group of guys before turning his attention back on me. He leans closer, wickedness gleaming in his eyes. "I'll suck your cock so hard, you'll forget your own name, much less what that bitch looked like."

My dick strains in my jeans. "You're poking the beast."

"Good. I hope he bites."

Oh, he fucking bites all right.

I stand up and lean in to whisper, making sure to grab his dick under the table through his jeans. "I'm going to go take a piss and settle my cock, boy. You're going to get our skins to go. Then, you're going straddle me in the cab of my truck while I fuck this hard cock with my hand and bite on that hot as fuck bottom lip. Are we clear?"

"Crystal."

"Good boy."

I rip at his shirt and my mouth fuses to his once more. The truck cab is dark, and our breaths fog up the windows. His dick is freed from his jeans like I promised it would be. I jerk at him, hard and unrelenting. He cries out when I bite hard on his bottom lip, tugging it.

"Pull my cock out," I instruct, my voice husky.

He fumbles at my jeans, then has my aching dick in his hot hand. Together, we jerk each other off, fast and frantically. It's frenzied—reminding me of when I came out of the closet in high school and had my first encounter with a guy. Xavi makes me feel young again. Not some bitter, grumpy cop who likes to top broken boys like him.

"Fuck," I hiss. "I'm about to come."

He works me harder, and then I'm moaning. My nuts seize up in pleasure. A growl escapes him before his own cum spurts out, soaking my hand. Once we're sated, I grab his discarded shirt and clean us up. I put him back in his jeans, and then do the same for myself. When he starts to slide off my lap, I grip his hips.

"I like you here," I tell him, pressing a kiss to his chest.

He relaxes, then runs his fingers through my hair. "I'm not used to all this yet."

"But you like it."

"I do."

I run my palms up the sides of his ribs, admiring his lean, muscular physique.

"Do you like being a cop?" he asks, his fingers scratching my scalp in an intimate way I've never experienced with anyone.

I don't cuddle.

With Xavi, though, I want to cuddle the fuck out of him.

"Since I was a kid."

"Now?"

I frown. I think about Frank Sanders. Shot in the fucking face by a man he pulled over for speeding. That shit disturbs me every time it happens.

"It's not as satisfying as it once was," I admit. I'm surprised to say those words. I haven't admitted that to anyone, not even Ronan or Joshua.

"Would you ever do anything else?"

"I've had some offers to do private security. The older I get, the more I consider it. Money sure is better," I say with a grunt. "Maybe one day."

"I can't imagine doing anything but singing from the fucking soul. Without my voice, I'm fucking no one."

I grip his jaw, our lips nearly touching. "Your music is a major part of you, but it's not you. You're deep, and you wear your heart on your sleeve. I've seen the way you talk about your bandmates. There's more to you than what you can do. I see you, boy."

He doesn't answer me, just kisses me hard. I can feel the smile against my mouth and vow to give him more praise. He fucking glows every time I give it.

Xavi Jacobs needs someone like me to pull him out of his hole, dust him off, and show him just how fucking amazing he is.

Not just someone.

Me.

9

Xavi

I'm antsy.

And stressed as hell.

He won't fuck me. I've been dying for it. Hell, he's been prepping me for it. I think I'm finally over the mental block of being with a guy. With Blaine, it doesn't feel gay or wrong, it just feels good. I wake up with his scent permeating around me and live to hear the deep gravelly timbre of his voice when he tells me good morning. I never knew I'd love such a simple routine—and with a man—but I do.

Which makes it incredibly difficult to know we're leaving today and haven't fucked.

What's wrong with me?

Did he change his mind?

Am I too shattered in the head?

"Toss your bags in the truck whenever you're ready to leave. I'll make us something to eat before we load up to get on the road." His command brokers no room for argument.

Fuck him.

Anger churns in my gut. It's a much easier pill to swallow than rejection.

You rejected Lex, asshole.

Yeah, and look where that landed him.

By tonight, my life will be business as usual. Nights spent with my friends and parties full of chicks wanting to get laid by any member in the hottest band in America. I'll go back to being under the microscope and popular as fuck.

That's who I am.

Xavi Jacobs, lead singer of Berlin Scandal.

Fucking hot.

Badass.

Fun.

Not this…

Not some fucking twink shacking up with a cop who feels sorry for him. Jesus. When I lay it out that way, I can see how pathetic I am. No wonder he doesn't want to fuck me. I wouldn't want to fuck me. I'd want to send me back on my way. Back to them. My people. The ones who love me for who they think I am—fucked up and ruined.

Blaine is not Lex.

Blaine is just a guy who thought he could mess around with me and got in over his head.

The rejection rages through me, hot and furious. I try to ignore it as I throw shit into the cab of his truck. Once I've loaded my bags, I chain smoke, my hands shaking violently. I'm thrumming with a wild energy building into something catastrophic. I hate that I feel helpless against it.

Thunder rumbles in the distance, and I inhale the scent of coming rain. It's so peaceful out here, and good for the soul. But now that I'm leaving, all my demons have run out to play with my emotions.

I need to go back in there and eat, but I can't face him.

Not when I feel like I'll fucking cry like a pussy.

It's real to me.

I want to scream it at Blaine like I never could to Lex.

But what happens when he tells me it was fun, but I'm too much for him? That it was great while it lasted, but he's ready to go back to his life—without me in it?

Rain starts pattering on my face. I turn my head up to take the abuse of the stinging pellets. The urge to burn, despite the forces of nature trying to put me out, is strong.

I yank my Zippo from my pocket, and for the first time since Blaine caught me with it, I flip it open with the intent to sear some control back into my senses. The moment the flame singes the hairs on my arm, something dark flashes forward, knocking the lighter from my hand. It hits the grass with a thud.

I'm left staring into violent eyes.

Oh shit.

I've never seen Blaine so…pissed.

"What the hell, Xa?" he growls, his voice not so different than the thunder behind him.

Clenching my jaw, I attempt to tear my stare from his. How do I explain the storm of emotions inside me? I don't fucking want to.

"Let's just go," I snap back.

"You look at me when we're talking, boy." His icy cold command forces my gaze to his. "That's better. Now, you're going to tell me why in the hell you developed an attitude problem in the last ten minutes."

"It doesn't fucking matter!" I roar, shoving him away from me, needing space and air and freedom.

"It matters to me," he snarls, rushing me again. His hands fist my shirt, and he shoves me against the side of his truck. "What happened?"

My throat aches.

It was real to me. That's what fucking happened.

"Boy, with the way your teeth are clenching, I can tell you're holding in a lot of shit you desperately need to say. Out with it."

The rain comes down harder, soaking us quickly to the bone.

"I'm homesick," I lie. "I just want to go home."

His nostrils flare. His eyes blaze with intensity. "That's how you want to play this?"

I lift my chin and glower at him. "Yep."

He grinds his hips against mine. My body reacts naturally after weeks of being with him. I'm hard. He's hard. We're both fired up and ready. Ready for something he won't give.

"I punish liars," he says, his eyes dropping to my lips. He moves his hips against mine, sending zings of pleasure splintering through me. "You want to be punished, Xa?"

Yes.

"No."

"I guess I have my answer." He trails soft kisses along my wet face to my neck. Then he bites me.

"Fuck!" I roar, trying and failing to shove the feral beast off me.

I feel his smile on my throat. Sadistic asshole. Then his mouth is sucking me hard like he does my dick. I groan. It feels good—too good. With just his lips on my neck and his dick grinding on mine, I'm starting to forget what I was mad about. All I feel is him. On me. Scorching inside me. His touch is addictive and thrilling.

Real.

I'm going to miss it.

I start to shove him away, but he yanks at the button of my jeans, then his hot hand is inside my pants, gripping my aching length. His jerks on my dick are painful and punishing, but I thrust against him eagerly. A low moan rumbles through me as my nuts seize up.

He releases me and steps back.

"What the fuck?" I gasp, my chest heaving.

"Get on your knees, boy, so I can fuck your face. Liars have to choke on cock before they can come."

Jesus, he is a filthy bastard.

I want to fight him on this. I want to demand to know what's happening. Why I'm not real enough for him. Instead, I drop to my knees, pulling at his button and zipper, eager to taste him. He hisses the moment I grip his length and lick his tip.

Thick, veiny, long.

I've dreamed about this fucking cock buried deep inside me for far too long. It's on the tip of my tongue to beg for it. When I look up at him, he grabs a handful of my hair with one hand, pulling so tight, it makes tears prickle in my eyes.

"Don't just look at it, Xa," he orders. "Suck on it. Taste it. Swallow me down. Understand?"

My lips part. *Fuck me, please.* He must sense my pleas because he shakes his head at me before guiding my mouth to his dick.

This is it.

A fucking goodbye.

Since this is probably the last dick I'll ever suck, I

throw every last ounce of me into giving him head. I suck and slurp and gag. I choke on his fat dick and squeeze at his balls. I scrape my teeth along his length and inhale his familiar scent. And when I hear him grunting in pleasure, I force him deep into my throat, trying desperately to ignore the way my muscles contract to reject his thickness.

"My fucking boy," he rasps out as he comes, hard and violent down my throat.

The heat burns my abused throat, but I take it. Sometimes goodbyes are bitter, but still fucking perfect. Once I swallow down the last of him, I stand on shaky legs, unable to meet his stare. He zips himself back up, then pounces on me.

"Your punishment," he growls as he grabs my dick and squeezes, "for lying is to look into my eyes while I make you come. I need to see all your truths, even if you fail to speak them."

Our eyes lock as he strokes me.

Pleasure. Pain.

Hate. Love.

Elation. Devastation.

Why won't you fuck me?

Why won't you love me?

His eyes never leave mine, forcing me to silently reveal all my inner secrets. The rain hides my tears, but it doesn't hide the pain. When my body trembles with the need to come, he strokes me hard until I release with a groan. My chin trembles. I don't know what to do.

I'm fucking losing it.

By this time tomorrow, I'll be officially lost.

His hand grips my jaw, and he kisses my wobbling lip until it stills. "Let's go home, boy. It's time."

Two weeks later…

I stare at the handful of pills in the chick's hands, but wave her off. "I said I'm not in the mood."

Owen's head snaps my way and he kisses the girl he's talking to before walking over to me. "Everything okay?"

"I just want him to party with me," the girl pouts.

"Beautiful, we're about to go onstage. Come find us after, yeah?" he says, turning on the charm.

She bats her lashes at him. "Sure thing, Owen."

"Can you give us a minute?" he asks.

Once she's gone, he grips my shoulders and leans his forehead to mine. "You've been different since you got back a couple weeks ago. Why won't you talk about it? What happened?"

I clench my jaw. "Nothing."

I'm not about to admit to one of my best friends

that I tried gay. Loved it. But then wasn't fucking good enough to stay that way. I wonder if that's how Lex felt. Bitterness churns in my gut. I want to get fucked up, but alone.

Just like Lex.

Tears threaten, and I pull away from my friend.

"Everyone out," Owen barks. "Right fucking now."

Seth and Riley are laser-focused on me. They start herding people out, leaving me alone with Owen. Great, I'm being tag-teamed with their shit.

"We're about to go on," I complain. "We can talk later."

"No," Owen says. "We're going to talk right now. I lost someone I loved because I blew them off. Not happening again."

My heart feels as though it's going to explode inside my chest.

"I loved him too," I bark out, my words boiling with emotion. "Not just you."

His gaze softens. "We all did, man. He was my brother. It crushed me when he died."

"He was my best friend…"

"And…" he implores.

"And what?" I roar, shoving him. "What the fuck do you mean 'and'?"

He glowers at me. "Stop bullshitting us, Xavi. Everyone knows you two had a thing."

Time stops. "A thing?"

"Fucking? Boyfriends? I don't know what the fuck it was!" He throws his hands in the air, his face turning red with anger.

I swing at him, but he ducks and points a warning finger at me.

"It was nothing!" I bellow. "Fucking nothing because of me!"

His brows furl together. "What do you mean?"

My shoulders slump. "He wanted to be more, and I let him down. I wasn't ready. Maybe if I'd been ready..."

Owen pounces on me, but not to hit me. I'm crushed in a brotherly hug. "Lex had fucking issues, man. You hear me? That was on him. He loved you, and you loved him. If he hadn't been fucked over his need for heroin, he'd have waited until you got there. Everyone knows this."

Everyone but me, apparently.

"I think I'm gay," I whisper, finally allowing it to break free. "I was with Blaine."

"I know, man. I know." He doesn't release me. "Why are you so scared to be happy?"

I squeeze my eyes shut. "Because it should have been with him."

"But it wasn't," he says softly. "You can still be happy with someone else."

"What about the band? Our image. You..." I trail off.

"You think I care about who you fuck? I just want you to smile once in a fucking while and mean it. I want you to crank out songs like the ones you wrote while at the cabin. I want my friend back—the guy who's been missing since my brother died."

"But people see Berlin Scandal and they see four guys who like to fuck girls."

He shakes his head as he pulls away. "No, dumbass. They see Berlin Scandal as the best rock band since Nirvana. What they hear is even more important. Soul in songs. Feelings and depth and a rawness you don't get from regular, mainstream shit. They hear our hearts bleeding because we all went through some fucked up shit—and our fans can relate to that, brother. Not who's hole we stick our dicks in. We're more than our sexual orientation. Jesus."

"I thought maybe you didn't like me and Lex being together because it was fucking with our fan-base..." It sounds pretty stupid, but it's true.

"I didn't like the idea of my druggie brother bringing down the lead singer of my band. Lex needed help, not a partner in crime. I was concerned when it came to his using. And with how close you two were, I worried with time you'd be using like him too."

Having Owen's acceptance is a huge relief. I didn't realize the agonizing weight crushing me until it'd been lifted.

"It's going to be a scandal when it gets out," I warn. "I can't do that to you guys."

"Fuck them," he growls. "Besides, that song is fucking amazing. They'll be more addicted to the new stuff than the fact that you like to suck dick."

I give him a playful shove. "Shut up, asshole."

His smile is crooked and boyish, reminding me of when we were just a couple kids with an idea to start a garage band. "My lips are sealed. I won't say anything until you're ready to tell people." His brow lifts. "So the cop, huh? Did he handcuff you to the bed?"

If only Blaine were that simple…

"Something like that," I admit, a smile tugging at my lips. But as soon as it breaches my face, it falls. "I think we're done."

"Hence the shitty attitude," he says. "And why are you suddenly done?"

My nostrils flare. I don't want to tell him, but it's Owen. "He won't fuck me."

"Maybe he likes taking it up the ass instead," he offers, waggling his eyebrows at me.

"No," I say with a frown. "I think I'm too much for him."

Owen scowls. "Bullshit. You're Xavi fucking Jacobs. Of course you're too much, but that's what makes you so fucking cool. His dick is broken if he doesn't want you."

I laugh. It feels weird talking about this shit with him, but freeing too. "I thought he wanted me. We did all kinds of kinky shit, but then it was time to come back home. I just…I don't know. He tried texting me, but I haven't replied."

Owen's hand grips my shoulder. "Did you talk to him or did you blow everything up to epic proportions like usual inside that fucking crazy head of yours?"

I flip him off.

"That's what I thought," he says. "After the show, call him. Take him on a fucking date or whatever the fuck. Just talk to him. Maybe it's you being a fucking freak like usual."

My heart stammers. "You think?"

"At least then you'll know. And if he's an asshole who doesn't want you, that's his loss. There's probably a world of hot gay dudes who would fall at your fucking feet the moment you tell everyone. You may bat for the opposite team, but I can guarantee you'll have a whole team show up with their bats ready to play."

I only want one bat.

I want Blaine on my team.

"Let's go, bros," Seth hollers, peeking his head inside the door. "You two fuckfaces can make out later. Right now, we have a club full of people to unveil our newest songs to."

Owen gives me a wink, and we head out.

The crowd for the small club is jam packed and insane. I'm soaked in sweat as we make it through our usual set and a couple new songs. The last song is the new one, "Burn." As soon as Riley starts pounding on the drums, I step up to the mic with my Gibson Les Paul and strum the first chord, finding myself thrust back to the cabin.

With him.

Long, hot, passionate nights.

Intimate conversations.

Being held and cared for.

Maybe I had misread things. It's not unusual for me to fuck everything up. Blaine doesn't seem the type to string people along or toy with them. He never once said he didn't want to see me when we got back.

I hate that hope stirs in my gut, but it fuels me on to sing my heart out.

"Burn...burn...burn..." I croon. "Why won't you let me burn?"

As I sing, I scan the sea of faces, feeling intensity coming from someone in particular. I seek out the heat like all those times I wanted the burn on my skin to fucking feel grounded in the moment. When my eyes lock on Blaine's, I nearly stop breathing. But I keep singing the song, trapped in his gaze.

A man in a suit leans in close and whispers something to Blaine. Blaine's hard look transforms into a beautiful one as he smiles. I jerk my gaze to the guy, glaring at him. My words become hard and raspy as I repeat, "Burn…burn…burn…"

The guy's hand is on his bicep.

Touching what's mine.

He's fucking mine.

Did Blaine think I pushed him away? That I don't want him anymore? Is he already dating someone else?

I finish the song and thank the audience.

And then I'm on the move.

"Get 'em!" Owen howls into the mic before thanking the fans some more and telling them we're headed back to the studio to record more songs like Burn.

As the crowd goes wild, I launch myself past the sea of people trying to throw themselves at me. I'm a man on a mission, and nothing will stop me.

When I make a break from the crowd and see Blaine perched at the bar with the handsy dude, I rush them. The guy's eyes widen when I approach, and he wisely jerks his hand back. My hot gaze lands on Blaine.

He fucking smirks.

Smug bastard.

"Mine," is all I say before grabbing his face with both hands and crashing my lips to his.

His hands are possessive as he clutches my ass, hauling me between his spread legs. Our kiss intensifies with need. He bites my lip, teasing me, but it's in a familiar, affectionate way that warms my fucking soul.

"About damn time you came to your senses, my boy."

My boy.

I'm fucking his, and he's fucking mine.

"I need you," I murmur against his mouth.

"And you're going to have me."

A chill shivers down my spine. Fucking finally.

10

Blaine

Rubbing his neck anxiously, Xavi paces the floor of my living room. After getting a firm nod from Joshua that it was okay to bail on him, I brought Xavi back to my place. The drive was torturous as hell, my dick ready to explode, but after Xavi checking his phone for the fifteenth time since he got inside the condo, all that heat has turned fucking ice cold.

"Everything okay?" I ask with a frown, slipping out of my jacket and loosening the buttons on my shirt.

It's been a couple weeks since we last spoke. I tried texting him, but got no reply. He clearly needed space. As much as it fucking killed me, I didn't chase him. I don't fucking chase people. I knew he would come to me when he was ready, and that happened to be a lot sooner than expected.

"We're trending," he says, shaking his head. "People took pictures of me kissing you."

My jaw tightens. "And?"

"And my fans are going wild."

"Bad wild?" I ask, turning my back to get a bottle of liquor from the cabinet. I still my movements when warm arms encompass me from behind.

"Good wild. They love the new songs and are hashtagging #XaviIsInLove."

My heart pounds in my chest. "And is it true?" My tone is gruff as I turn and grasp his face, darting his eyes to mine. "Are you in love, boy?"

"I promised myself after Lex I wouldn't ever lie if I was asked that question."

"So don't lie," I prompt.

"Fucking madly," he growls.

"Fucking madly," I echo, crashing my lips to his and backing him across the room to my bedroom. Pulling away from his lips, I nip and tease the skin of his neck. I tear his shirt in half, littering the floor with the material.

"I want to know what it's like," he pants.

"What what's like?" I growl, yanking open his jeans and shoving him backward onto the bed.

"What it's like to have you completely."

"Tell me exactly what you want, boy," I rumble, tearing off my clothes and tugging his jeans from him.

"I want you to fuck me."

127

Those magic fucking words are like music to my ears. I flash him a wicked smile.

Pulling open the bedside drawer, I take out a bottle of lube. "You're a good boy, but I'm going to fuck you like you're a bad one."

His breathing elevates, and his cock strains, creamy liquid coating the tip. I lather up my cock with lube, giving the length a couple long, firm strokes. Snagging Xavi's ankle, I lift his leg over my shoulder and lean in to ravish his mouth with mine, taking my time dueling with his tongue. His hands explore the planes of my body as I fist his cock, moving to his balls and then stroking a finger down the crease of his ass. I test his hole with a prod, and he accepts me greedily. I stretch him, preparing the muscles for my hard, fat cock. Sitting back, I take his ankles into my hands and spread his legs.

"Stroke that pretty dick for me," I tell him.

Long fingers curl around his girth, massaging. I line my cock up with his asshole and tip my hips forward, breaching the rings of muscle there.

"Fuck, fuck," he hisses.

"It's just pressure. Relax and let me in, boy," I command. "Let me fucking love you."

Licking his lips, his head bobs manically as his hand furiously fists his dick. He likes the pain with pleasure. I piston my hips, pushing my cock in farther.

"More," he begs.

Releasing his ankles, I collapse over him, catching my fall with my arms and resting them each side of his head. I look into his glazed brown eyes as I sink all the way into him. Our mutual moans fill the room.

A frenzy takes us over, lips crashing, hands pulling and groping. I punish him with hard, manic thrusts, my balls slapping against his ass cheeks as my dick burrows inside him. We fuck, we dance, we sing, we make love. Sweat creates a mist over our skin, allowing me to glide over him.

"Turn over," I growl into his ear, slipping my cock out of him, mourning the loss of his warmth around me.

Obeying, he flips over onto his stomach, lifting his ass.

I kiss down his back, lapping up the scent of his sweat and nibbling his ass cheeks, leaving my mark. My tongue teases the crack and swirls his asshole before I straighten, line my cock back up with his hole, and thrust forward.

Grabbing his hips, I pound into him, my release beckoning. He's so tight, the muscles of his anus caress my cock with each plunge. Curling my hand around his waist, I grip his hand that's stroking his cock, and I help pump him until we both cry out our release.

We collapse on the bed, panting as we come down.

"That was worth the wait, boy." I grin, dragging him over my chest and dropping a kiss to head.

"Sure was, perv."

Three weeks later...

Sitting across from Joshua at his club, Hush, I eyeball the scratches around his neck and the cut on his lip. "You need to tell me something?"

A sly grin tugs up the side of his face. "I don't fuck and tell, you know that."

It's not like him to enjoy the rough edge games, but hey, who am I to judge?

"You decided what you're going to do about Ronan's offer?" he asks, checking his phone.

Sighing, I swirl the drink in my bottle and tap my fingers on the table. "He made an offer that's hard to refuse. I mean, going with my boy for the three months he's touring is the cherry on the creamy fucking frosting." I wink.

"He finally found your price?" He chuckles, drinking his whiskey.

"My work can be mentally draining. It might do me good to step away for a while. I can always go back."

"So, fulltime bodyguard for the band while they tour next year," he says with a whistle. "You've had worse jobs."

Jabbing him in the arm, I check my watch and throw some cash on the table before getting to my feet. He always argues when I try to pay for drinks at his club, but I always win that battle. I wave him goodbye and head down the corridor to the private room I've booked for the night. I rap my knuckles on the wood and wait. The door clicks open, and there he fucking is, right on time.

Xavi Jacobs, lead singer of Berlin Scandal, and my fucking boy.

"Hey, perv," Xavi rumbles.

"That's going to cost you, boy."

His eyes dart to the wall lined with paddles, whips, and crops. "A spanking?"

I smirk as I let the door close behind me. "You know me better than that. Nothing is ever that simple." I reach forward and unbutton his jeans. "Pull these down to your knees, then put your hands on the wall."

"Are you going to arrest me, officer?" he taunts, his dark eyes flickering with wickedness.

"That's detective to you, son. Now, assume the position before you make this ten times worse."

With his eyes on mine, he shoves his jeans down his thighs. It fucking gets me hard every time he goes commando. Knowing he's free-balling whenever we go out is maddening. His cock juts out at me. He presses his palms to the wall and looks over his shoulder with that haughty smirk he's perfected.

It's like he loves to push and disobey just so I'll set him straight.

We're a match made in hell.

Playfully, I smack his ass cheek. "Don't look at me. Eyes forward or this will get much worse for you."

"Oooh, I'm scared," he sasses. Fucking brat.

Ignoring his taunting, I grip his hips, making him step farther away from the wall, then guide his hands down so he's nearly bent in half. "These," I murmur as I reach between his spread thighs and gently massage his balls, "should be scared." With those words, I pop his nut sack.

He howls, clenching his ass. "Motherfucker!"

"Keep mouthing off," I warn.

His grumbles are kept under his breath. Good boy. Leaving him for the moment, I walk over to the wall and consider my choices. He loves a good old fashioned ass whipping. The more it stings and burns, the better for my masochistic boy. I select a long crop with leather fringe at the end. Paddles are fun, but I'm looking for something more precise. Smirking, I make my way back over to him and toss the crop on the bed before stripping down, then pick it up once more.

"I won't go easy on you," I tell him, gently caressing his ass cheek.

"You never do."

"I'm going to whip the fuck out of you, and then you're going to ride my dick like a good boy. You're going to lube your ass up while I watch, climb on, and show me how good you can fuck. And if I think you're slacking off, I'm going to smack your pretty dick and watch you cry."

"I won't fucking cry," he growls.

"I'll make you cry." A sinister grin spreads across my face. "And then you'll come because you love the pain, boy. You love it so fucking much. That even when you're crying and your dick is in so much pain, you'll spurt all over my chest because that's what good boys do."

"Fuck off," he rumbles.

God, he really knows the buttons to push to get my dick hard and the urge to punish him overwhelming.

Whap!

The crop slices through the air, between his thighs, slapping his nut sac, making him scream. I fucking love his screams. Digging my fingers in his hip to hold him still, I strike him again, this time on the back of his thigh. He squirms and curses, but he never takes his hands from the wall. To reward him, I rub my finger between his cheeks, teasing his hole, then smack his ass with the crop.

Whap!
Whap!
Whap!

I watch with delight as red stripes crisscross his pale flesh. So fucking beautiful. When my dick is seeping with the need to be inside him, I toss the crop to the floor and step back.

"You know what I want," I growl as I lie back on the bed.

He trembles as he removes the rest of his clothing. His dick is hard and bobbing, the tip glistening with pre-cum. He picks up the Hush complimentary pouch of lube and tears it open with his teeth. My gaze sears into him as I watch him pour it all over his fingers and then reach behind himself to get it ready.

"Show me, boy," I order.

His eyes flicker with heat before he turns around. I watch with satisfaction as he fingerfucks his asshole. When he adds a second finger, I groan.

"Good," I croon. "Now come sit on my cock where you belong."

He pulls his fingers out, then straddles me on the bed. I stroke his cock as he grips my dick to ease himself down over my length.

"Fuck me good," I instruct. "I want to see your dick bouncing."

Just like when he's on stage, he rocks his hips and dances to songs that only play inside his head. So fucking hot and mine. I still can't believe it. My eyes take in his perfect form and the way his lower abs flex each time he moves his body over mine.

"Faster," I command, desperate to see him lose control.

With his naughty gaze on mine, he slows it to a teasing crawl.

"Bad boy," I snarl.

I smack his dick, making his ass clench around my cock.

"Fuck!" he hisses. "Fuck!"

"Faster then."

He stays steady, taunting and teasing.

I slap his dick harder, and he cries out and starts to pull away, but I grip his hips, forcing him to fuck me faster. His fingers dig into my chest as he gives in and starts moving quicker. With his eyes closed and his mouth parted, he looks like a fucking angel. I've never seen anything so fucking gorgeous in all my life.

"Come here and kiss me, boy," I beg, hating how needy I sound.

He flashes me the sweetest of smiles. "I love you, Blaine."

Our lips crash together, a chaotic thrashing of tongues, lips, and teeth. He owns me heart and soul with one kiss, while I own his body and mind with mine. We're a perfect pair, creating something fucking magical together.

I'm about to come, so I reach between us and jerk him right into ecstasy. The moment he moans, his ass clenching around my dick, I come with a groan. I fill him up, and when I'm wrung dry, I yank him to me. My cock softens and slips out of him, my seed leaking out all over the fucking place.

We're a mess, but cleaning up my dirty boy is always the best part. I hug him to me and kiss his sweaty head, holding him close to my heart where he belongs.

"Love you too, Xa. Always will."

He relaxes against me. It fills me with pride that he lets go of all the pressures of the world and all his inner chaos when we're together. He frees himself for me, and oh what a gift it is. There have been many men in my past, but not one compares to Xavi Jacobs. He's feeling and beauty and eroticism and music all wrapped into a broken, sexy-as-sin boy.

I may share him during the day with the world— the one he's designed for them to see.

But every night, I get Xa. The real him. Free, vulnerable, unsure. He's given me the softest parts of him and trusted me to take care of him.

He's my boy.

He'll always be my boy.

EPILOGUE

Xavi

Two months later...

*Y*ou *cut me open.*
Filled me up with you.
Never needed stitches, 'cause you're the fuckin' glue.

I smirk, imagining Sofina echoing those words with me. It'll sound sweet with her velvety voice dripping like honey all over those dark lyrics. Us coming together for a collaboration was one of Ronan's best ideas yet.

Sofina is fucking brilliant. What started as a dinner between friends quickly turned into a brainstorming session in Ronan's kitchen. We playfully started singing one of her songs, then one of mine, and then we sort of blended them, jiving off each other. Ronan's eyes were fucking huge when he and Blaine came in not long after.

And so our collab was born.

We've decided to write something new, she and I. We're going to record two versions—a power ballad, high vocals version, then one with the boys, complete with drums, bass, and heavy guitar riffs. It was our idea to do two of the same songs, recorded differently to try to market them to both the rock and pop crowds. Ronan was true to his word. I proved to him I could stay off drugs and out of trouble, and he renegotiated our contract. "Burn" was just a glimpse of what I could do, and he knew that.

It's been number one for eight weeks straight with no signs of moving from the top spot.

Ever since that night at Sofina's bar, it caught fire and has blazed bright since.

You rip me apart and I don't care.

Everywhere. You're everywhere.

I scribble down the newest possible lyrics. Tonight, I'll suck Blaine's dick, then ask for the password to the wireless Wi-Fi access point he brought with us in case Ronan needs to be in touch. We're at the cabin, which he likes to keep technology free, but sometimes if I work him just right, he calls me a good boy and gives me whatever the fuck I want. Tonight, I just want to Facetime with my new friend Sofina and see what she thinks.

"Usually when you smirk like that, you're about to get into trouble," Blaine says as he shuts the front door behind him.

I'm stunned stupid at the sight of him. He's been out front chopping wood like a fuckin' lumberjack since a winter storm is said to be coming this week. But my hot-blooded man is drenched in sweat and had long-lost his fitted Henley. My mouth waters as I take in his ripped, tattooed muscles.

Fuck, he's hot.

"What?" he asks, arching a brow and rubbing his palm down his chiseled abs. "Like something you see?"

I laugh. "You're an asshole. You do this shit on purpose, don't you? Distract me from work."

"We come here so you'll play too," he says, his dark eyes gleaming with wickedness.

Rising from the couch, I toss the notebook aside and stalk over to him. His masculine scent—salty with a hint of pine—makes me thirsty to lick every inch of wetness from him. I settle for a heated kiss that has him gripping my ass hard.

"I think I could take a break to play," I tease, nipping at his bottom lip.

He pulls away, grinning. "Let me shower first. Stay right here like a good boy. I'll be back."

As soon as he turns to go upstairs, I roll my eyes. I watch his back muscles flex as he walks up the steps, and I check out his ass. Stay. Yeah fucking right.

I rip off my shirt and prowl after him. Never will I get enough of this man. It still freaks me out sometimes that I've given up on pussy to settle for one dick. When I'm feeling low, it messes with my head a little. But all it takes is a kiss from Blaine to send my heart ratcheting through my chest. He chases away all the unease and confusion, filling me with certainty and him. Together, we fit. We're fucking perfect. I don't have to prove it to the world, just him. And every day, I work hard to show Blaine I'm a man worth having.

It turns out, Owen was also right. Our fans don't care who I love. Women still want me, and so do men. But more than that, they want our music.

The sound of the shower running greets me the moment I enter our room. Blaine is already naked and stepping under the spray. I strip out of my clothes, hot on his heels. When I make it under the hot spray, he shakes his head at me.

"You disobeyed me, boy."

He loves it.

Fucker loves punishing me, so I'm a good boy if we're being fucking frank. I'm giving him what he wants. The chance to whip me into submission in a way that gets both our dicks hard.

"I'm a rebel," I tell him with a grin as I grab the soap. "Can I make it up to you?"

His eyes darken as he nods. I start soaping his chest, running my fingers along the grooves of his V muscles, purposefully touching him everywhere but his hard-as-stone cock.

"You're a tease," he growls.

"You like it."

He doesn't argue. When I forcefully turn him around, he laughs, the rich sound echoing in the shower. Playfully, I smack his wet ass.

"Maybe I'm going to be in charge this time," I taunt.

"Cute," he grunts. "Really fucking cute."

I hug him from behind, rubbing my dick between the crack of his ass. "You're going to take it, boy," I mock in a deep voice. "Every long inch."

He growls.

The soap slips from my grip and hits the floor.

"Pick it up, boy," I order, pretending to sound like him. "Pick it up so I can fuck your tight hole."

I'm spun around so fast and slammed against the shower wall, I'm surprised he doesn't send us through the glass. His eyes are fire and lust, burning wildly as he grips my throat tight. Our dicks are hard, sandwiched between us, wet and soapy.

"You're in trouble now," he warns, his eyes dipping to look down at my mouth.

I lick my lips and grin. "Good. Now punish me so I can get the Wi-Fi password."

The corner of his mouth twitches, and I mentally high-five myself for almost getting him to smile after I've pissed him off. He quickly schools his features and grabs my wrist with his other hand, guiding it to his hot cock.

"You're going to have to earn it, boy."

I jack him off under the water, washing away the remnants of the soap, then drop to my knees, my eyes never leaving his. He grips a handful of my hair and hisses the moment I tease his tip with my tongue.

As I take him deep in my mouth, I can't help but feel at peace. Blaine was everything I never knew I needed. He somehow knew and was drawn to me. And he forced me to face things I may never have been able to do on my own.

Now he owns every part of me.

He thrusts hard, sliding easily into my throat and making my muscles constrict. My mind dances with all the possibilities of how he'll take me tonight. All night. Hard, brutal, relentless. And at the end of the night, we'll fall together in a mess of sweaty limbs and whispered I love yous.

Sorry, Sof, no work tonight.

I'm about to be a bad boy and play with my man.

All. Night. Long.

Darting my eyes up to Blaine's, I flash him an evil look before scraping my teeth along his dick.

"That right there will get you in trouble," he growls.

Pulling off his cock, I smirk. "A spanking?"

His eyes narrow. "Use your imagination, boy."

My mind reels with a million things he could do to me. All dark, devious, and hot as hell.

I can't fucking wait.

The End

PLAY ME

Up Next!

*From international bestselling authors, **Ker Dukey and K Webster** comes a **fast-paced**, hot, **instalove** standalone **lunchtime read** from their KKinky Reads collection!*

BOOKS BY
KER DUKEY & K WEBSTER

Pretty Little Dolls Series:
Pretty Stolen Dolls
Pretty Lost Dolls
Pretty New Doll
Pretty Broken Dolls

The V Games Series:
Vlad
Ven
Vas

KKinky Reads Collection:
Share Me
Choke Me
Daddy Me
Watch Me
Hurt Me

The Elite Seven Series:
Lust by Ker Dukey
Pride by J.D. Hollyfield
Wrath by Claire C. Riley
Envy by MN Forgy
Gluttony by K Webster
Sloth by Giana Darling
Greed by Ker Dukey and K Webster

Four Fathers Series:
Blackstone by J.D. Hollyfield
Kingston by Dani Rene
Pearson by K Webster
Wheeler by Ker Dukey

Four Sons Series:
Nixon by Ker Dukey
Hayden by J.D. Hollfield
Brock by Dani Rene
Camden by K Webster

ACKNOWLEDGEMENTS

Thank you to our hottie husbands. Baby Daddy and Mr. Webster are the real inspirations...even in this book...especially in this book...

Ker and K love each other and would normally use this section to thank each other, but they like to save the real thanks when they're alone on video chat...

A huge thank you to our reader groups. You all are insanely supportive and we can't thank you enough.

Thanks so much to Terrie Arasin and Misty Walker! Two of the best PAs everrrr! We love you ladies!

A gigantic thank you to those who always help K out. Elizabeth Clinton, Ella Stewart, Misty Walker, Holly Sparks, Jillian Ruize, Gina Behrends, Wendy Rinebold and Nikki Ash—you ladies are amazing!

Great thanks to Ker's awesome ladies for helping make this book is as awesome as can be! Couldn't have done it without you: Ashley Cestra, Rosa Saucedo, PA Allison, Teresa Nicholson, and KimBookJunkie.

A big thank you to our author friends who have given

us your friendship and your support. You have no idea how much that means to us.

Thank you to all of our blogger friends both big and small that go above and beyond to always share our stuff. You all rock! #AllBlogsMatter

Monica with Word Nerd Editing, thank you SO much for editing this book. You rock!!

Thank you Stacey Blake for being amazing as always when formatting our books and in general. We love you!

Lastly but certainly not least of all, thank you to all of the wonderful readers out there who are willing to hear our stories and enjoy the characters like we do. It means the world to us!

ABOUT THE AUTHORS

KER DUKEY

My books all tend to be darker romance, the edge of your seat, angst-filled reads. My advice to my readers when starting one of my titles... prepare for the unexpected.

I have always had a passion for storytelling, whether it be through lyrics or bedtime stories with my sisters growing up.

My mom would always have a book in her hand when I was young and passed on her love for reading, inspiring me to venture into writing my own. Not all love stories are made from light- some are created in darkness but are just as powerful and worth telling.

When I'm not lost in the world of characters, I love spending time with my family. I'm a mom and that comes first in my life, but when I do get down time, I love attending music concerts or reading events with my younger sister.

News Letter sign up: eepurl.com/OpJxT

Website: authorkerdukey.com

Facebook: www.facebook.com/KerDukeyauthor

Twitter: twitter.com/KerDukeyauthor

Instagram: www.instagram.com/kerdukey

BookBub: www.bookbub.com/profile/ker-dukey

Goodreads: www.goodreads.com/author/show/7313508.
Ker_Dukey

Contact me here:
Ker: Kerryduke34@gmail.com
Ker's PA: terriesin@gmail.com

K WEBSTER

K Webster is a *USA Today* Bestselling author. Her titles have claimed many bestseller tags in numerous categories, are translated in multiple languages, and have been adapted into audiobooks. She lives in "Tornado Alley" with her husband, two children, and her baby dog named Blue. When she's not writing, she's reading, drinking copious amounts of coffee, and researching aliens.

Facebook:www.facebook.com/authorkwebster

Blog:authorkwebster.wordpress.com

Twitter:twitter.com/KristiWebster

Email:kristi@authorkwebster.com

Goodreads:www.goodreads.com/user/show/10439773-k-webster

Instagram:instagram.com/kristiwebster

KKINKY READS

COLLECTION

There's only one of her and
they all want a piece.

SHARE *me*

A REVERSE HAREM STORY

BESTSELLING AUTHORS

KER DUKEY
K WEBSTER

SHARE Me

They have one job.

Keep me safe.

But none of us are safe against the allure we have when we're together.

Control and professionalism used to be something they prided themselves on.

But now that we're secluded and alone, lines blur and control quickly loses to need.

Someone is trying to snuff out my life, but they may not get the chance if I'm devoured whole by my saviors first.

This is a fiery-hot mfmmm romance sure to make you self-combust! A perfect combination of sweet and sexy with a smidgen of suspense! You'll get a happy ending that'll make you swoon!

How long can she
hold her breath?

CHOKE
Me

bestselling authors
KER DUKEY & K WEBSTER

CHOKE Me

I had a plan.
Make Ren Hayes pay.
But plans don't always turn out the way we want them to.

He was found not guilty of murdering my best friend.
But that doesn't make him innocent.
In my eyes, he's guilty.

Guilty of charming everyone around him into believing his
innocence.
Guilty of being so intoxicating I forget who he is—what he
is.
And guilty of awakening parts of me I never knew existed
before his touch.

I know eventually, I'll succumb.
His allure beckons me.
Keeping me on the edge of madness between lust and hate.

In the end, it's me who's guilty.
Guilty of allowing him to take my breath away.

This is a super steamy romance sure to take your breath
away! A perfect combination of sweet and sexy with a
smidgen of suspense that you can gobble up in just an hour
or two! You'll get a happy ending that'll make you swoon!

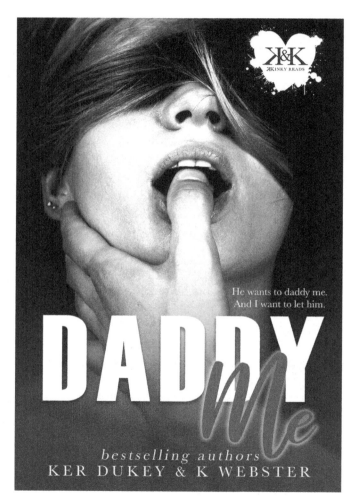

He wants to daddy me.
And I want to let him.

DADDY
Me

bestselling authors
KER DUKEY & K WEBSTER

DADDY *Me*

Dreams are supposed to be encouraged.
Not mine.
My brother likes to keep me on a tight leash, tethered to
an unexceptional life.
But when Ronan Hayes walks into our family-owned bar,
he opens my cage and offers me freedom.

Ronan wants to give me the world.
A chance to take flight and soar.
He sees something special in me, and I want nothing more
than to be that for him.
Special.

He's my dream maker.
My shot. My hope. My everything.

Ronan craves to take care of me.
A protector. A confidant. A provider. A lover.
He wants to daddy me.
And I want to let him.

She likes it when
I watch her.

WATCH
Me

bestselling authors
KER DUKEY & K WEBSTER

WATCH

I like to watch.

It's a compulsion I can't stop.
Now, my desire is centered around one woman.
My obsession borders on stalking, but the glass wall keeps me in check.

She can't see my face, yet she dances in an intensely erotic and intimate way that feels designed just for me.
She likes when I watch her.

But things are about to change when she waltzes out of that room and into my tattoo parlor, turning my world completely upside down.

There's no glass wall this time.

Made in the USA
Columbia, SC
01 September 2019